A Tuscan Dream

A Contemporary Romance Novel

Lucy Appadoo

This book is dedicated to those who have struggled in relationships. The fight for love is worth it.

Contents

1. DREAMS   1

2. A WORK TRIP (4 WEEKS LATER)   8

3. FIRST DAY   15

4. A MEETING   20

5. CONNECTION   27

6. A DINNER   33

7. ATTRACTION   38

8. SUPPLIES   43

9. DANCE MOVES   48

10. MEMORIES   52

11. DINING IN STYLE   57

12. WINERY TOUR   63

13. CURIOSITY   67

14. A RELEASE   72

15. INSIGHT   78

16. AN APOLOGY   82

17. A JOURNEY   86

18. MEMORIES   94

19. A STOLEN KISS   100

20. INTIMACY   106

21. AWKWARD MORNING   112

22. BANTER   116

23. KEEPING IT CASUAL   122

24. SUPPRESSION   130

25. A STERN WORD   135

26. ANGER   140

27. A PERSPECTIVE   145

28. JEALOUSY   149

29. MISTAKE   153

30. RUMINATIONS   158

31. OVERSEAS OFFER   162

32. CRAVING   168

33. DETACHED   174

34. MOVING ON   178

35. THE VILLA OPENING   182

36. MELBOURNE ARRIVAL   187

37. EPILOGUE (TWO WEEKS LATER)   189

ABOUT THE AUTHOR   194

ALSO BY LUCY APPADOO   195

Chapter 1

DREAMS

S itting inside her manager's office, Alessandra De Luca angled her head she worked as an interior designer. "What did you say, Sandy?"

"Our celebrity client, Flavio, has asked us to design his house in Tuscany, and you leave in a month if you agree to it," said Sandy, drawing a manicured nail through her blonde hair. She inched forward at her desk, waiting for a response.

Alessandra's heart lifted at the thought of heading back to her country of origin. It had always been a dream to go back. "And he's decided that I should be the one to design his villa? In Italy?" She shook her head. "Surely there are other designers to choose from. Why me?"

Sandy raised an eyebrow. "You underestimate yourself, Alessandra. These past six years you've been with the company have done wonders for your reputation. Each year, you excel in your work and improve." She clasped her hands together. "He read about you in those few articles commending you for your work, and he would like to work with you. What do you say? Are you up to going to Siena for at least four months? It might be longer, taking into account delays and progress of the work."

Alessandra remembered the rolling hills of Tuscany and the old vineyards. Her family first moved from Pisa, Italy to Coburg, Australia when she was ten. Now, she lived in her own terrace-style home in Carlton. "Of course, I'll go. You don't need to ask twice, Sandy. Oh, this is such a dream come true. I—"

Sandy put up a hand. "Okay, I cannot keep up with what you are saying. Slow down and take a pause. I need to give you a run-down of what's happening."

Alessandra squirmed in her seat and subdued her enthusiasm. "Sorry. Go ahead."

Sandy nodded and fiddled with papers in a manila folder. "The place where Flavio would like the villa built will be in Montepulciano in Siena on a huge block of land. Apparently it's easier to build on a large block to avoid any changes in Italy's laws if you plan to extend a home later. Anyway, I'm going off track." She opened the manila folder. "Flavio's brother, Giuseppe, is the builder you'll be working with. He lives in Siena and will be overseeing the project." She paused. "You will be working with the renowned architect, Romeo."

She drew back. "Romeo? Not *the* Romeo Bianchi, the famous architect who's won awards for a whole range of overseas projects? Not that Romeo, surely?"

Sandy nodded. "Yes, it's that Romeo. He is heading out to Tuscany at nine o'clock tonight to begin the work. You'll meet the team there in a month as construction starts." She exhaled. "There are two apartments in Montepulciano that the team will be lodging at, and mostly everything has been paid for. Some food supplies will be available in the apartment, but they will eventually run out and you'll need to buy your own. Oh, and one more thing."

Now that she realised she'd be working with a cold-hearted, arrogant playboy, Alessandra felt less enthusiastic. "What is it?"

Sandy hesitated when a knock at the door caused her to peer at it. "Romeo Bianchi is here. Flavio insisted you two meet before you work together." She got up and opened the door.

Alessandra ran her hands through her hair and shifted nervously in her seat. She wrung her hands as her breathing accelerated.

Slowly turning around, she forced a smile as Romeo walked into the office with his posture as straight as a post and a mouth set in a line.

Sandy brought over a chair and put it next to hers. "Mr Bianchi. This is our esteemed interior designer, Alessandra De Luca. Alessandra, this is Romeo Bianchi."

He nodded. "A pleasure to meet you."

"And you too." The architect's arrogant air permeated the room, overshadowing his attractiveness. No depth of colour in those hard green eyes, nor his broad, muscular form could transcend that arrogance. Inwardly groaning, Alessandra forced herself to relax. It was going to be a long four months.

Romeo Bianchi sat on the chair beside this woman, Alessandra. He couldn't believe he had to work with a woman too boisterous and loud for his liking. A woman who undoubtedly would give him headaches while they liaised on the project. When he'd heard he was working with her, he had done his research on his future co-worker. He needed to know what type of person she was to ensure they could do their best work together. Romeo couldn't afford mistakes. The article he'd read about her was accompanied by photos of her tightly hugging her colleagues, posing in a flamboyant way, and smirking at the camera at an awards party. Even the dress she wore was much too short for the viewing public. Dread settled in his core.

Oh, sure. She was attractive with her olive skin tone, maroon spiral shoulder-length hair, and striking eyes, but he wasn't fooled by her beauty. She would probably be too distracted and scattered to do a great job on this villa, but he would make sure she adhered to all the rules of law and the highest standards.

He focused on Sandy. "I am heading out to Tuscany tonight, whereafter your...Alessandra over here will join me in a month's time."

"Great. Alessandra is looking forward to the experience," said Sandy.

He turned to Alessandra. "By that time, you will have studied the shape of the villa and have an idea of how the space works with the interior. Have you dealt with large-scale projects overseas before?"

Alessandra stiffened in her seat. "No, I haven't, but I have done huge scale commercial projects around Australia. This will be my first overseas experience. I am grateful to Flavio for his generous proposal."

A bead of sweat formed behind his neck. "Hmm. I can steer you in the right direction when it comes to Italy. We have to follow different regulations and protocols than Australia of course, and the exceptions to rules can be somewhat confusing at times."

Alessandra nodded. "I assure you, Mr Bianchi, that I am committed to doing my best work on this project. I cannot wait to get a start on it."

"Yes, but remember that the rules are different in Italy, and things may take longer to complete, given that we are a fair way from the city of Siena. It will take longer to secure supplies, and we might not need an interior designer until much later than a month away."

Sandy intervened. "I understand what you are saying, Mr Bianchi, but Flavio has a schedule he plans to follow, and he would like the two of you to work together in a month. Besides, architects and interior designers work together from the ground up all the time. We've occasionally liaised that way, and if there is an amicable working relationship between both of you, I don't see the problem in Alessandra coming to Tuscany in a month's time."

He rubbed his hands together, squinting. "Fair enough. This is quite an important project, with increasing pressure. We are building a villa for a celebrity. Fortunate for us, Flavio cannot get enough of buying houses in different parts of the world. It could mean more work. It could mean we make a name for ourselves."

Alessandra's eyes darkened. "I have everyone's interests at heart, and I will do an amazing job on the home, Mr Bianchi. Do not doubt that."

Alessandra sat on the edge of her bed. Her best friend, Mimi, was helping sort through clothes to pack for Italy.

Mimi's hazel eyes rested on a pair of shorts on the bed. She drew a hand through her long, glossy, sandy hair that reached her lower back. Her friend resembled a top model, and every time she walked into a room people stared. "Tell me about this Romeo guy. What's he really like?"

She shook her head, wondering why the man rubbed her the wrong way. She focused on a plain red blouse in her pile to take to Italy. "I don't know about this top. Should I bring this one? I'm not sure why I bought it. The cleavage is too low."

Mimi picked up the top and put it on the Italy pile. "Hell, yes. I love this top, and why not flaunt your gorgeous body, girl? It's great for the evening. Now answer my question about Romeo."

"He's arrogant, vain, stern, and too serious for my liking. He's all about rules and protocols, and I can see he'll be a hard taskmaster. I wish I'd never met him because now I dread this working trip. I was so excited but I'm thinking we won't work well together."

Mimi sighed. "Oh, come on, Lessi. Don't judge the man from one meeting. Even if you do, he is so easy on the eyes. And those lips? My God. Maybe you should introduce us." She frowned. "I might surprise you in the next couple of months with a visit. Have fun in Italy and don't think too much. Do your job and you will excel, girl."

"Maybe you're right. But I get the impression he's going to give me a hard time. I mean, he's already judging me and we haven't even started." She picked up a pair of shorts. "Should I take these to Italy?"

Mimi nodded. "Why not? If it's hot over there, you won't need to be wearing office attire. Besides, you'll no doubt have time to check out the sights too, won't you?"

"Possibly, but I wonder if the washing facilities are any good or whether we'll have enough water to wash clothes."

"Oh, come on. This is a new time and things have advanced, even in Italy. I am sure Flavio will not spare any expense to cater to your needs and those of Romeo. Now tell me, is he as hot in person as he is on the news?"

Alessandra sighed. "Oh, please. Can we talk about something else? Let's finish this sorting. Then we'll go shopping for a few more pieces I need. Are you free later today?"

Mimi grinned. "Of course, girl. I'm all yours. I am so going to miss you when you leave for all those months. Make sure you video chat me as often as you can."

Alessandra shifted and hugged her friend. Mimi had been there during her family struggles and her boyfriend challenges. They had been friends since high school. Though Alessandra adored her life in Australia, she'd still had a part of Italy in her heart. It was hard to shake. The short ten years that she'd lived in Pisa had enchanted her memories and made her yearn to return.

Chapter 2

A WORK TRIP (4 WEEKS LATER)

A lessandra claimed her baggage at the airport in Florence. Wheeling her suitcase with her travel bag slung over her shoulder, she searched for Giuseppe at the exit doors. She took a breath and stopped, her eyes roaming the international airport. Where was he? If she didn't find him soon, she'd have to catch a taxi to her destination.

Taking a few steps forward, she finally spotted a man with brown eyes who held a sign with her name on it. She approached the short, paunchy man, who appeared to be in his fifties, and was beaming from ear to ear.

"Hello. You must be Alessandra." He shook her hand. "I'm Giuseppe, the contractor, and your driver for today. Welcome to Florence."

"Hi, Giuseppe. Good to meet you." He took the suitcase from her and turned away. "Follow me."

His car was parked near the taxi ranks, and they walked in silence until reaching it. He hefted her suitcase and travel bag into the boot, and she entered the passenger's side. The humidity hit her when she opened the window as Giuseppe pulled out into traffic. Quite a contrast from the winter weather in Melbourne. "Make yourself comfortable because we're in for a long drive to Montepulciano."

"How long will it take?" She turned to him briefly, tearing her gaze away from trying to glimpse the city beyond the busy airport traffic.

He turned to her briefly then returned his attention to the road. "It depends on the traffic but at least an hour and a half."

Alessandra focused on the rows of congested city buildings in hues of brown, cream, red, dirty grey, and light yellow against a backdrop of the Apennine mountains in the distance as they sped past. Car horns and trucks blared, and people riding mopeds moved dangerously close to cars. She smelled smoke and petrol fumes, mixed in with the aroma of fresh spices and herbs. As the car passed a small chapel, she tracked the progression of people crossing the narrow roads, busy on their way or joining crowds gathering through the city centre cafes and restaurants. She was curious about how the next four months of her life would pan out.

Giuseppe brought her out of her reverie. "I am so excited to be working with you, Alessandra. We do have a few subcontractors we're working with, and Romeo, of course. He is the best of the best in the business. How about you? Is this your first time travelling to Italy?"

She rested back in her seat. "I lived in Pisa up until I was ten years old. My family moved to Melbourne for a better life and more opportunities."

He nodded. "Does your family live with you in Australia now? They have never been back here?"

She shook her head. "No, we've been in Melbourne all these years, and it is amazing to be back. I'm realising how much I've missed Italy and its history."

"No doubt you will have the opportunity to travel around Tuscany. There will be times when you will need to wait for construction of different parts of the house."

"I might just do that." She would like to visit other parts of Tuscany, and might even extend her stay after she finished with this project.

Alessandra got out of the car, taking in the medieval hilltop town of Montepulciano. She breathed in the sweet, woody fragrance of fern, and the heat feathered her face making her sweat. Her heart warmed at the natural green surrounds, the hills and valleys covered with olive groves, rows of grape vines and forests of pine and chestnut trees. The varied shades of green landscape fell below the backdrop of the clear, blue skies and the shadows of the hills. It gave her a sense of vastness and space, and she could imagine flying around this beautiful natural landscape. The range of humble estates, mountains, and different shades of green and cream encouraged her to seek out other parts of Siena.

Giuseppe retrieved her suitcase and travel bag, then put them next to a caravan situated on the side of the villa. He led her to the worksite, the villa in its frame stage with its foundation laid. At least fifteen men rushed around the site. The buzz of a drill and the chink of a hammer from a corner of the building site echoed as they worked on the structure. She followed Giuseppe to the other side of the site. The caravan must be where the contractors had their breaks before going home. Several cars surrounded the caravan, and she assumed that some of the contractors might live in the area or in Siena, which was at least an hour away.

She didn't know yet where she'd be staying, but was jolted out of wondering about it when she

spotted the back of a man she recognised.

Giuseppe greeted the man. "Romeo! Our new designer is here."

Perspiration dripped from the back of Romeo's neck. He held a clipboard and continued to scrutinise the area before turning to them. He nodded. "Yes, we've already met, Giuseppe. Pleasure, Alessandra."

Alessandra swallowed, her throat dry. His clipped tone didn't give the impression it was a pleasure. "Hello Romeo. I can see you are busy."

Giuseppe beamed at her then led her around the site to introduce her to the subcontractors. They greeted her warmly. "I will leave you here with Romeo to discuss today's plans, then he can take you to the apartment where you'll stay. It's not far from here."

"Thanks, Giuseppe. I appreciate you driving me."

Giuseppe nodded then made himself scarce, disappearing into the worksite, picking up a hammer and placing a hard hat on his head on the way. Alessandra had no idea what to do, so she stood there awkwardly until she found Romeo gazing at her.

"I will let you settle in first then we'll start on the plan for the villa tomorrow. You might need to take a short nap and get some rest."

"Where will I be staying?"

He held his clipboard against his chest. "An apartment owned by Flavio. One of the contractors, Geraldo, sleeps in the caravan, and the rest of them are rooming in another apartment nearby. Given that we are meant to be working together, the others thought it made sense to have us remain in one place." He averted his eyes and she wondered what he truly thought about that arrangement. She winced at the idea of staying with a man who was too serious and detached for her liking, but she would make do.

He walked to one of the cars, a white Fiat Panda, without indicating that she should follow him. She hurried to collect her bags from near the caravan, and Romeo briskly grabbed them out of her hands, stuffing them in the boot. Without a word, he climbed into the driver's seat. She let herself into the car and sat beside him, buckling in just as he pulled off the site.

Romeo pulled the suitcase from the boot of his rental car. Alessandra waited for him as he wheeled it to the front door of the apartment, which was a five-minute drive from the building site.

He'd been in Italy for the past month and had dreaded the day that Alessandra would join him. She most likely expected a silver platter at her feet without understanding what it was like to work diligently. The fancy clothes and cascades of bling around her neck and wrists reflecting the light blinded him. He had met her kind before.

He unlocked and opened the door to the air-conditioned interior. "We have two bedrooms down that corridor." He wheeled the suitcase along the rustic floorboards, passing the living room and resting it near the bed. "This is your room." He turned to her. "I can show you the kitchen if you need to eat or drink."

Alessandra nodded. "I could use a glass of water." She followed him out to the kitchen where Romeo reached high for a glass and filled it with cold water from the fridge. He placed it on the table. She took a seat on one of the four padded chairs. "Has the construction been working to deadlines so far?"

Romeo nodded and sat across from her, not wishing to become too comfortable, as he needed to return to the site to check on measurements. The contractors had already miscalculated the space in the kitchen area and he didn't need a repeat mistake. "We have had a few delays with errors, but it happens." Despite needing to be as far away from the woman as possible and returning to work, he didn't want to leave the cool interior of the apartment. Once he left, he'd be faced with the blasted heat again. He hated summer and preferred the cool of winter. At least then he could work without sweaty armpits.

Alessandra beamed. "Flavio's an interesting man, isn't he? I only spoke to him on the phone once, and he is extremely generous. I appreciate this apartment he's given us, but to manage the upkeep of both apartments, plus the villa he's building. Well, it is expensive."

He wondered if she even knew the value of money, flaunting her own money with her fancy clothes, make-up, and jewellery. "He is an extremely hard worker and has achieved a lot. I commend the man for putting his money into wise investment decisions. He might have the upkeep and expenses, but he rents out these apartments at other times, so he makes his money back. As for the villa, he has worked hard to construct a luxurious home, and I'm going to make sure it's the best home it can possibly be."

Alessandra inched forward. "I understand he works hard and I assumed he would rent out these apartments. But they still need maintenance when he's not here to oversee things." She gazed into her lap, and for a moment, he was curious about her true thoughts. Did she truly appreciate Flavio's generous nature or would she take advantage of his generosity? He needed this project to work, and he hoped she followed his rules so they could have an amicable working relationship.

He stood up. "I have to head back to the site. As I said earlier, I imagine you will need to rest before your big first day of work tomorrow." Not waiting for a reply, Romeo left her.

Alessandra sighed, shaking her head at the man who had probably never shown an ounce of emotion in his life. She couldn't believe she had to work with him. He was cold and aloof, and she wondered if he had a heart beating in his chest. How would they work together when they were complete opposites? He didn't even know her and had already judged her.

Brushing off her irritation, she rose and surveyed the apartment. The kitchen featured a long, brown timber table and four padded chairs including the one she had perched on. A cooktop stood beside a glossy counter and dishwasher with brown, rustic cupboards underneath. Overhead crème cupboards and a stainless-steel fridge completed the space. Brick adorned one wall in the living space and a TV hung above a timber unit. Colourful throw pillows were placed around the red cotton sofa, and in front of it stood a low rustic coffee table. A narrow corridor with cathedral ceilings led to the bedrooms.

Alessandra drank down a few more glasses of water before heading to her bedroom, plonking herself underneath the bedsheets and falling into a deep sleep.

Chapter 3

FIRST DAY

Jetlag had Alessandra sleeping until the next morning, still wearing the same clothes. Her arms and the back of her neck sweated after having the air conditioner off overnight. She yawned and rubbed her eyes then looked at the wall clock above the bed. It was only five o'clock in the morning. How could she have slept all afternoon and night without having any dinner? She was famished, her stomach grumbling as she rose. After rummaging in her suitcase, she changed into a light, white blouse then found a peach silk skirt. Her hands ran over the silky fabric as she zipped it behind her.

Walking into the bathroom, she splashed cold water over her face and dried it with a towel from a rack. Peering into the mirror, she frowned at her dishevelled naturally spiral hair that ran down to her shoulders. She drew a hand through it to give it some style. Oh, who cared anyway? It wasn't like she had anyone to impress here.

Exiting the bathroom, she walked to the kitchen and opened the fridge. She found a range of fruits including a rockmelon, honeydew, strawberries, apricots, and peaches inside several bowls. Selecting strawberries, an apricot, and a peach, she washed them and found a plate in one of the cupboards. As she sat down, she bit into a straw-berry.

A fresh-faced Romeo headed down the hall towards her. He was wearing a tight-fitted black t-shirt with black sweatpants and jogging shoes. His expression was one of coldness, frowning as if she had no right to eat the fruit.

"Morning," Romeo said in a monotone. He opened the pantry door and pulled out two slices of bread. Putting them into a toaster by the sink, he turned to her. "You slept forever yesterday."

Was it a crime to sleep? What did he expect from her after a twen-ty-four-hour flight? "I guess I was tired after a full day's flight." She swallowed a bite of apricot. "Who supplied all the food here?"

Romeo sat at the far end of the table and dug into his buttered toast. Wiping the remnants of crumbs from his lips with a finger, he gazed at her. "Flavio's housekeeper came by and stocked the fridge and freezer. She comes initially whenever he has occupants in the apartment. Whenever it runs out, it will be our responsibility to stock the fridge. I can take you to the supermarket." He wiped his lips then sipped on a glass of water. "I take it you don't have an international licence to drive here?"

Alessandra shook her head. "No, I didn't have the desire to drive around Italy, given the way I remember how they drove when I was younger." She could have cursed herself at sharing that information. If he was going to be standoffish, why did she have to share her past with him? He must not have realised what she said considering his silence, so she carried on. "What's on the agenda for today?"

He drank down his remaining water and rested his back against the chair, sizing her up again. "We'll have to make decisions about the floor space. Flavio gave us free rein to design the space as we like, and Giuseppe's been nominated to approve most things. They're brothers, so he has an idea what Flavio likes and dislikes. Anything he is not sure about, will go through Flavio."

Alessandra nodded. "You're up early. Is this the time you usually wake up?"

He rose from the table. "I like to go for a short sprint before heading to the site. It clears my head." He pressed his lips together and washed his kitchen items. "We leave at seven-thirty so make sure you're ready." Rushing out of the apartment, he left her speechless. *So arrogant!*

Romeo ran around a path through a park, fighting his thoughts of Alessandra. His mind kept returning to her mindfully chewing the strawberry with those full lips. That blouse she wore revealed a tad of cleavage. She could pass as a model but he didn't need the distraction. He had a job to do, and this project was important both to his reputation and his goal. No, he refused to have any more images of Alessandra.

Last night, the silence in the apartment got to him, and part of him wanted to talk to someone. Sure, there were times he hung out with his friend, Mike, or the other contractors, but he couldn't do that every night. He did not need to confide in the woman. Rest assured; he was on the ball meeting deadlines at each phase of construction.

He stopped jogging and bowed his head to catch his breath as he walked back inside the apartment. It had been an hour since he'd spoken to Alessandra, and as he opened the door, he stopped short at three words he heard coming from her mouth. "He is arrogant, Mia, and..."

Romeo greeted her. "Hello. The arrogant one is back." The expression on Alessandra's expression was priceless as she turned to him with wide eyes and pale face.

Speaking into her laptop, she whispered, "I have to go."

Romeo shook his head, glaring at her. "I have to shower. Be ready to leave when I'm done." He headed into his bedroom, slamming drawers. Throwing his fresh clothes inside the bathroom, Romeo shut the door behind him. His chest tightened and his back ached. The woman was the Devil incarnate. What was Flavio thinking?

Alessandra's heart raced, a rush of guilt hitting her as she realised how much worse she'd made her working relationship. He now had more reasons to despise her, and she'd have to work that much harder to win him over. But then again, why would she need to win him over? Romeo was a jerk. What did she care whether he liked her or not? Her work spoke for itself, and she didn't need to prove herself to him, but only to Flavio and future clients.

She walked to her room, picking up her black satchel and handbag. Alessandra retrieved her sketch pad, laptop, assorted rulers, measuring tape, and markers to prepare her design brief once she'd checked out the space at the site.

She scrolled through her mobile phone and messages, then jolted when a voice made her turn.

"Ready?" She nodded. "Let's go." He hurried ahead to the front door and out to the rental car. The short trip to the site was quiet and tense, and Alessandra doubted he'd ever forgive her for calling him arrogant, even if it was true. No matter what, she'd be the ever-professional and fulfil her mission. This job was important to her and could help her break into new markets and increase her clientele.

Chapter 4

A MEETING

Alessandra clasped her hands together inside the caravan where they held their design meeting with Giuseppe. The caravan had grey, linoleum flooring with a low, black marble table near a sink with drawers, and a cooktop to the left appeared clean. There was a double bed with a grey quilt cover against the back wall, and two chairs at the glossy table.

Romeo sat across from her, unrolling his blueprint and spreading it on the table. "This here is the design that Flavio agreed to before you arrived." He glanced at Alessandra. One of the workers walked inside, but she couldn't remember his name. His towering height barely squeezed into the space, and his dark eyes scanned her. A scar above his right eyebrow was prominent.

Giuseppe nodded in the man's direction. "Hey, Mike." He turned to Alessandra. "He's the best carpenter in the business and has worked hard to move things along. He's also Romeo's best friend."

Mike beamed at Alessandra. "How's it going, Alessandra?

Romeo's scowl deepened and his eyes locked on his friend, who was grinning in her direction. Didn't he like Mike being friendly with her? Romeo better not make this any more difficult than it had to be.

"I'm ready to get started, Mike. I can see how hard you've been working. It is going to be great." Alessandra returned Mike's grin and a polite nod.

He shrugged. "It'll take a while yet, but we were on track until today." He faced Romeo. "Marco put one of the beams in the bedroom area in the wrong spot. We can leave it in, make the alterations here." He pointed to the blueprint.

Romeo squinted. "Absolutely not, Mike. This has been approved by the council the way it is. You have to move it. It is not going to put a dent in the progression of work. Make sure it's done."

Giuseppe shifted. "I agree with Romeo. Fix it."

Mike nodded. "Sure thing, boss." He turned to Alessandra. "How's your first day so far, Alessandra? I don't understand why you'd want to work with this one. A hard taskmaster." Mike pointed at Romeo.

She warmed to him. Clearly, Mike understood Romeo's coldness, and that made her believe he wouldn't hold whatever Romeo told the man against her. "All okay, and thanks for the heads up, Mike. I'm a hard worker myself and absolutely love what I do. Learning about the client is incredibly important. When I understand what the client wants, I can make sure their home appears and feels pleasing in ways unique to them."

"Your reputation speaks for itself. You must be proud of your work." If only Romeo could be this friendly. "It's great to meet you again." He faced the others. "I'll talk to all of you later."

When Mike exited the caravan, Romeo pointed to his architectural design. "The villa is going to have five bedrooms in the main house and a cottage on the right side over here. The first floor will feature two of the bedrooms with ensuite rooms, and an attached bathroom with a tub." She moved in, scrutinising the complex design. "The cottage will have two bedrooms, and the rooms will have full air conditioning and ceiling fans. Flavio said he wants a rustic atmosphere, so here there'll be a rustic sitting room. And over here, the plan is to have a bar and billiards room, a gym, and a cosy library with a fireplace. He plans to have a fireplace in the main living room here as well."

Alessandra pointed to another part of the design. "What's this space here? A study area? But there's also another room here."

Romeo nodded. "Yes, and the study will have an indoor games area beside it."

Alessandra rubbed her hands, wondering whether four months would be enough time to complete everything. She doubted it, given the complexity of his design. "The kitchen here is pretty spacious too. It seems as though Flavio plans to do a lot of entertaining."

Giuseppe chuckled. "Flavio has friends from all parts of the globe, yes. And what he wants is a rustic, Art Nouveau style design. Have you designed such a huge project before?"

Alessandra winced. Would they judge her simply because she hadn't had the experience of designing a huge villa, period, let alone overseas? "No, but I've had loads of experience with federation-style homes and cottages. I have plenty of ideas and I can put together specs once I can buy a few samples."

Romeo sighed. "It is a large-scale project and needs our complete focus."

Alessandra's chest tightened and her throat dried up. "I understand that, and it will be. This project is important to me."

He averted his eyes. "This project is important to all of us. I mean, we need to follow the rules and adhere to the plan."

Alessandra swallowed, part of her wishing she could tell him to stick his rules. Another part wanted to leave the caravan and crawl under a rock. She did neither. "Giuseppe. I needed to show you something." She rummaged in her satchel with a shaky hand, ignoring the ache in her stomach, and showed Giuseppe her colour wheel. "To get a sense of style, I need to first work with themes of colours. I plan to work with one room at a time, but in terms of the colours, do you have an idea of Flavio's preferences? I assume pastel, colourful shades?"

Giuseppe glared at Romeo, picked up the colour wheel, exploring the various shades. "You would be right, Alessandra. Flavio likes these different shades of orange or pink, with a few light peach to red tones. Like these."

Alessandra nodded. "Thanks. I will work with these colour schemes and tell you what I come up with." She jotted down a few notes in her notebook and put away the colour wheel.

Giuseppe got up, gesturing with his hands. "Come up with a design and I'll let my brother know. Once he gives me his approval, we can take it from there." Mike knocked on the door and came in. It was Mike again. "Yes," said Giuseppe.

Mike waved him over. "A problem. Need you for a minute."

Giuseppe sighed, gave Romeo a strange look, then rose. "Excuse me. Duty calls."

The room suddenly felt empty without Giuseppe, and she briefly turned to Romeo before staring at the design and making rough sketches in her sketch pad. She lay a finger on the plan. "If the kitchen had more space, we could fit a bigger table here and leave extra room for overhead cabinets. As it stands, it comes across as a little crammed."

Romeo stiffened. "I have designed this according to what Flavio wanted, and as architecture is within my expertise, my design stands. Your designs will have to work around mine, given I have been here longer than you. I am certain Flavio would agree."

She clenched her hands. "I have a sofa in mind for the living room, but the position of the door here with the wall is all wrong. We need to optimise the space. Can you shift the location of the door and put it here instead?" Alessandra pointed but Romeo sat back, cross-armed, squinting, with his lips pressed together. Waiting in vain for a response, she looked away and jotted more notes on her pad. It was going to be a long day.

Romeo flinched every time she put her dainty fingers on his designs. How dare she question his blueprint? The nerve of her questioning him. "Listen, if we make too many changes to this design, it might trigger a call for permits. And do you realise how long that could take in Italy? You will have to work within these specifications or as close as possible to them. If you had been here earlier, then we could have agreed on things then."

"That couldn't be helped, Romeo. I had another project to finish. Is there any chance of a compromise?"

Romeo's neck ached and he had a migraine. Rising, he poured himself a glass of water then turned to her. "I don't suppose you would like a drink of water?"

Alessandra nodded. "I would love one. Thank you."

He retrieved a glass from the upper cabinet and poured water from the tap. "Here you go." He put it down roughly beside her, spilling a few drops. She frowned, and he spotted the lightest tinge of red in her dark eyes, no doubt still tired from the flight. She had dimples, he realized, with naturally spiral hair to her shoulders, high cheekbones, and thick eyelashes. She had a slight Italian accent too, which made her sound mysterious. What was he doing? She was against his work and he wouldn't be taken in by her beauty.

"Listen. We need to work together on this. Let's take a walk on the site. It'll give me a sense of the space in the rooms. If I am not asking you to move any walls, then I don't see a problem with us compromising on some of your measurements."

Romeo waited for Alessandra to drink down her water, then rose and rolled up the blueprints. "How do you work?"

"As I said, I get a feel for the place, then I create a plan in my sketchbook and do a mock-up on my laptop, using computer-aided design software."

Did she need to spell it out as if he didn't understand what CAD was? He refrained from a sarcastic response and walked outside the caravan, hoping she would follow. The blast of heat hit him like a tornado as she moved ahead of him, aware of the feminine curve of her hips, and well-toned arms and legs underneath her peach skirt. His heart raced, but he pushed his thoughts aside as they reached the worksite.

Alessandra walked ahead of Romeo around the building site, noting the beams and frames supporting most areas of the house. The blaring of drills, hammering, and chainsaws reverberated in her brain as she held her sketchpad and made rough drawings of what to position in the different rooms, visualising the space, flooring, and furnishings.

Romeo turned to her. "I take it you'll show me your elevation drawings for the cabinets and bathroom layout?"

"Of course. I will transfer my ideas to CAD and do it in stages." She walked alongside him to the bathroom area, watching the way his swagger brought out his muscular and toned legs in the tightness of his jeans and heavy biceps displayed by his t-shirt. The luscious shape of his mouth made her wonder how many women he had kissed. Shaking away these unwelcome images in her head, Alessandra took a breath and refocused. Jotting down more notes in both her notepad and sketchpad, she moved on ahead to the billiards and games room. This seemed like a monumental task, but she was up for the challenge.

Working until lunchtime, Romeo stopped by a delivery van. A middle-aged man carried out a basket of ready-made rolls and Romeo took them from him. "Let's go inside for food," he said to Alessandra.

They entered the caravan. He handed one roll to each of the contractors, who were taking a quick break. As he gave her a roll, their hands brushed. A tingle spread throughout her arms.

"Thanks, Romeo."

"The local shop makes tasty rolls. We have certain privileges with a movie star as a client."

Mike stood by Alessandra. "Has Romeo given you a hard time, or been too territorial? He is like that sometimes."

Romeo shoved his friend playfully. "Hey, man. You are dead to me now. Dead."

Alessandra watched the two friends banter with one another and realised how close they were. Mike brought out a pleasant side to Romeo, but she obviously brought out his worst side. The other workers—fifteen of them—made small talk with her and were easy-going. She expected being left out as the only woman, but surprisingly, they included her and treated her with respect. Well, all except for one man.

Chapter 5

CONNECTION

A few days later, Alessandra walked around a craft market to source materials after Romeo had driven her to Siena. The drive over there was tense, and he had his radio on full blast as if he wasn't in the mood to talk.

She ran her fingers over fabrics lying on rickety tables then bought a few samples of window furnishings to give Giuseppe a selection. She passed by aisles, Romeo following a few feet behind her, and bought a few more knick-knacks.

Romeo approached her as they made their way to the exit. "Giuseppe mentioned a ceramics shop you would like nearby."

"Sure. Let's go. Is it walking distance?"

"I'll drive." He rushed on ahead. The drive was only a few minutes, and Romeo parked behind the Duomo at Via Fusari. She remembered coming to Siena with her mother in better days before she left them. Bitter-sweet memories of her mother holding her hand and laughing when a young Alessandra dropped her ice cream flickered through her mind. Her mother had quickly bought her another one, and she remembered the mixture of flavours, and how safe she'd felt when her mother had taken her for a piggyback ride. Not long after that memory, her mother had left her. She fought back tears and a constricted chest, barely able to breathe.

They both leapt out of the car and headed inside the ceramics shop. A woman with short hair, wearing a black singlet top sat at a table with a thin brush in her hand. She painted the outer edge of a plate, creating an intricate pattern of stars. Covering the table were plastic jars of assorted paint colours and unpainted ceramic bowls and coffee cups. The shop itself displayed rows upon rows of shelves featuring square and round plates, bowls, and cups and saucers with an array of colourful designs, including mandala and sun designs, stars, and flowery decorations.

Romeo stood by her, watching the woman carefully paint the plate until she put it aside and started on a small cup. His aftershave was musky, and she broke out of her reverie when the woman glanced up.

The woman grinned. "Hello. How about a gift for your wife, sir?"

Romeo's face turned red as he avoided Alessandra's eyes. "She is not my wife."

Alessandra stuck to business. "I would love to buy some of these plates. Do you sell a lot of these?"

The woman put down her brush and rose. "Why, of course. It's been part of the family business for a couple of generations. Just yesterday, we shipped a few pieces to America and to different parts of Italy. What would you like?"

Alessandra walked over to the counter. She accidentally bumped into Romeo, ignoring a tingle in her stomach. He moved aside as she roamed the shelves. "I like these two and that bowl. Oh, also this square plate and round plate. I am in the process of designing a home for someone else and would like to buy a few samples to show him."

The woman nodded. "Here, take my brochure. We have a website you can look at too." She boxed up the items and Alessandra swiped her card.

Romeo and Alessandra wandered down the streets, exploring fabric shops and local handcraft stores. They gawked at a local craftsman making a piece of woodwork featuring a mother holding her cute baby, with such detail in the carving. Alessandra later bought intricate souvenirs and a decorative bookend for herself.

He had misjudged Alessandra, realising now that she knew her stuff and had a lot of creative thoughts. He didn't much appreciate her boisterous, emotional nature, but for the sake of the project, they probably could cooperate.

Passing by a cafe, he turned to her. "Are you hungry?"

Alessandra nodded. "I guess I could eat. Why not?" She walked with him inside the cafe, a tiny, crowded space.

The space was dark and elongated, with a row of tables on one side and a few couches on the other. Coffee, cinnamon, and spices filled the air. The walls displayed photos of groups of people and the landscape of Tuscany, with its green, hilly terrain and surrounding villages.

After placing their order, Romeo sat back against the chair and became curious about what made Alessandra tick. She was an enigma he wanted to discover, purely for work reasons. If they could be compatible, he could move on to bigger and better projects.

The elderly waiter brought them their drinks of an iced coffee and a beer for him.

He became speechless when Alessandra dug into her strawberry which had been set on top of a dollop of cream. The berry reddened her lips. Overcome with a strange desire to reach over and wipe it off, he instead turned away, sipping on his beer. He needed a distraction and wondered when they'd have their food.

"With that subtle accent I take it you were you born in Italy?"

Alessandra dabbed her mouth with a napkin and gazed at him curiously. "Yes, I lived in Pisa with my family and moved to Australia when I was ten. I had an advanced primary school education in Italy and found I had to skip a grade when I was in high school. But I remember coming to Siena with...anyway, it has brought back a few memories. What about you? With the name Bianchi I assume you're Italian too?"

He nodded. "Yes, my parents are Italian-born but I was born in Melbourne. I have been to Italy three times with either my family or for work reasons. I never tire of coming to this beautiful place. The buildings, the architecture. Tuscany, especially."

"It does have that magic. I feel nostalgic at times, but I love Australia too."

He nodded. "Flavio is a man of heart. I've had projects with other celebrities and have that experience, but you can never tire of returning to Italy."

She nodded. "Have you always been an architect?"

He gripped his glass. "I wouldn't dream of doing anything else. Each project is so unique, and I thrive on the challenge of doing a huge villa with a cottage beside it." It was his dream to make more of a name for himself.

The waiter brought their orders of garlic focaccia and thick chips for Romeo, and bruschetta and a salad for Alessandra.

They dug into their meals in silence, and Romeo savoured the crisp to soft texture and yeasty, richness of his bread. Alessandra dove into her bruschetta, and he briefly noticed her tongue wrap around the bread while she scanned the swarm of people in the cafe. It was almost sensual the way she ate. What was wrong with him? Chiding himself, Romeo chalked up his observations to boredom, loneliness, and the romantic atmosphere of Italy. He was not attracted to Alessandra.

Alessandra caught Romeo watching her, and she wondered if she was eating with her mouth open. Conscious of how she was eating now, she ate slower, capturing the way Romeo wrapped his lips around a chip, and how his square jaw became even more prominent as he chewed sensually. Why did he have to be so attractive and smart? It would be easier to hate him for his arrogance without any other redeemable qualities. Italy must be getting to her. She didn't want a relationship. Didn't trust men. They couldn't commit. No, she was better off being single and not risking her heart or self-esteem because of a man—especially one as arrogant and cold as Romeo.

She had to distract herself from his lips. "You and Mike seem tight."

He wiped his mouth and sipped his beer. Putting down his glass, he said, "We've been best friends since primary school, and he often works with me on buildings. I don't know any other carpenters who do a fine job as he does."

"I guess you complement each other with your varying skills; you as the mental professional and he as the hands-on guy."

"I happen to get my hands dirty too. I don't mind doing handy work every now and then. I have made a couple of bookshelves and a chest of drawers. Whether I make them durable enough is questionable, though. What about you? Any other skills besides interior decorating?"

His eyes bore into hers. Self-conscious, she felt her cleavage was far too visible. She played with the top of her t-shirt. "I like to cook, and I've done public speaking." She wondered if she did more public speaking, could she make an even bigger name of her work? "I am hoping to start my own interior design business in the near future." How did she let her goal slip? She hadn't intended to say so much to him.

He nodded. "Right. I guess this work will give you a chance to reach those ambitions, but we need to agree on things for the sake of the project." He frowned. "These public speaking gigs. Do you have any on social media?"

"No, they were never publicised that way. Only small events that weren't televised or recorded on anyone's website or social media, thank God. I am not that interesting."

Half an hour later, Romeo finished off his second beer. "Are you ready to leave?"

"Of course. I can't wait to show Giuseppe my samples. Hopefully, Flavio likes one of the selections. We'll see."

As they walked out of the cafe, Alessandra thought they might just be able to get along as colleagues.

Chapter 6

A DINNER

Romeo dug into warm lasagne at Giuseppe's home in Montepulciano, not very far from the building site, a few days later. The cheesy, meaty texture was heaven in his stomach as he captured the rich flavours and soft texture in his mouth.

Giuseppe's wife, Enza, had invited him over for dinner. Much to Romeo's disappointment, Alessandra had also been invited. He had been with her enough at work, and now he had to share his nights with her as well. It wasn't as if he hadn't enjoyed their outing in Siena a little, but he needed his space. She was a distraction he didn't need when all he was meant to do was build the best villa in all of Italy. Besides, she had called him arrogant behind his back, and he couldn't forget that so easily. She might have played nice, but beneath that mask of hers, she was like all the others. No doubt, she would stab you in the back as soon as she got the chance. All women did. He had seen a dark streak in fleeting moments on her face, and he wasn't interested in unlocking that side of her.

No, Romeo refused to be taken in by her beauty and extroverted nature. If they could tolerate each other for long enough to finish their venture, all the better. But he didn't need to be with her outside work too.

Enza broke into his reverie. "Are you not liking my lasagne, dear?" She drew a hand through her grey fringe, the rest of her black hair tied up in a low bun. Her brown eyes assessed him with curiosity.

He gave her a reassuring smile. "I am sorry, Enza. Of course, I am. I've just been thinking about this new job of ours." He held his fork in the air. "I need to give my Mum this recipe. I am sure you've got a secret sauce."

Enza chuckled and waved her hand around. "Oh, yes. My grand-mother from Pisa showed me how to blend all the right ingredients. But I would be happy to write it down for your mother." She turned to Alessandra. "Giuseppe told me your family comes from Pisa. Have you visited there lately?"

Alessandra shook her head, her face reddening. "No, not since I was ten years old, but I do plan to visit once I've finished with this design. Take some leave from work. It is a little overdue."

Giuseppe intervened as he finished chewing the pasta then set down his fork. "Your parents must be missing their old country. No doubt they would like to visit one day."

Alessandra shifted and she avoided his eyes. "Could I use your bathroom?"

Enza gave Giuseppe a strange look. "Of course, dear." She pointed behind her. "It's past the living room and down to your right."

Alessandra rushed out of her seat, and Romeo wondered why her mood had changed. He couldn't help notice the way his had chest tightened at her reaction, curiosity getting the better of him.

Giuseppe took a sip of his homemade wine then broke off a piece of bread. "Did I say something wrong, Romeo? I didn't mean to wander into her business, but I like to make conversation."

Romeo shrugged. "You did nothing wrong, Giuseppe. Maybe it reminded her of something. I don't know her very well."

Enza had a cheeky grin on her face. "Oh, but you would like to know her. Wouldn't you, Romeo? She is very beautiful and smart too."

Romeo's throat turned dry. "I hadn't realised, Enza."

Giuseppe shook his head and touched her tenderly on the shoulder. "Enza, darling. Leave the man alone. Why do you always have to go playing matchmaker?"

Enza sighed. "Oh, come on, darling. Any hot-blooded male would be aware of how striking she is and how much of a soft heart she has. But I can tell that under that strong, vibrant veneer, she is a lost little girl. She is troubled by something but hides it well. Don't you think, Romeo?"

He was becoming tired of this conversation, but he didn't want to be rude. "I can see that she is approximately five-foot-nine-inches, has large brown eyes, spiral hair down to her shoulders, an olive complexion, and is fit and toned. Other than that, I wouldn't have a clue. And I don't wish to. I have a job to do and it is all I can focus on." Checking to make sure Alessandra wasn't returning yet, Romeo said, "I don't have any interest in her whatsoever. She is purely a business colleague and it's all she will ever be, Enza." He had been friends with Giuseppe and Enza for at least five years, but they could be stubborn with their own ideas at times. When he didn't see them, he often video chatted with them. They were like family.

Enza nodded. "Hmm. Whatever you say, Romeo."

He turned at the sound of light footsteps and his heart skipped a beat at Alessandra's return. Had she heard their conversation?

Alessandra pushed aside her dark thoughts about her mother and splashed on a bubbly grin. She was experienced at faking it, and right now, she had to be strong. Why let that mother of hers ruin her night? She could move on to a lighter subject. Alessandra faced Enza. "Giuseppe tells me you have two teenage children."

Enza beamed. "Yes, my daughter Maria is seventeen and my son, Alfonzo, is eighteen. They have gone out to a nightclub with their friends. But they are together, and Alfonzo always keeps an eye out on Maria. He will keep her safe."

Alessandra nodded. "That's great. When you're young, you need to go out and have fun. Smell the beautiful air here in Tuscany. I imagine they go out often?"

Giuseppe sighed. "Too often for my liking. I swear the day Maria brings a man home will be the day I disown her."

Romeo laughed. "Yes, there are a lot of people out there you can't trust. But Maria has a good head on her shoulders and Alfonzo is watching out for her. He will protect her."

Alessandra couldn't believe how antiquated that sounded. "They can watch out for each other." The nerve of the man.

Romeo forked a meatball from a huge pot in the middle of the table. "Giuseppe, Mike would like me to choose flooring. I'll be out most of the day tomorrow."

Giuseppe nodded. "Why don't you take Alessandra with you? She can offer you amazing input for flooring, I'm sure."

Romeo knit his brows. "I believe Mike and I have it under control. Alessandra will have enough to do with creating the design model and deciding on more of the fabrics."

"But flooring is my department as much as it is yours, Romeo," said Alessandra.

Enza shook her head. "Now, now, Romeo. You should be working together on flooring as two heads can be better than one."

Giuseppe pressed his lips together. He poured sauce over his meat, then took a bite of the meatball. "It's settled then. Take Alessandra with you so you can talk through more of what works."

Romeo turned quiet and forked meat to his mouth. He wiped his face with a napkin.

What was his problem? They had had a pleasant time when they went to Siena, and now he was treating her like the enemy again. It was as much her assignment as it was his, and she had every right to help choose the right flooring. It had to complement everything in the home.

Half an hour later, they sat in the living room sipping wine and enjoying tiramisu. Romeo all but ignored her until he scowled at her. "You have cream on your face."

"Oh, thanks." She picked up a napkin and wiped her chin while Romeo's eyes lingered on her mouth. When she caught him staring, he focused on Enza and Giuseppe snuggled together on the couch. Alessandra and Romeo sat across from each other on armchairs. She was curious about what it would be like to love a man she trusted as Enza did with Giuseppe. No, she would never find a man like that when they had all turned on her. She was better off being single.

Chapter 7

ATTRACTION

When they arrived at the apartment after their dinner out with Guiseppe and Enza, Alessandra hurried inside and picked up her laptop from the coffee table. "I have to video chat with my family and friend." She was about to enter her room when Romeo grunted behind her then poured water from the tap. She realised that mentioning her friend might have reminded him of how she'd called him arrogant the other day. She had to fix this, as she didn't want it hanging over their heads.

"We need to talk," said Alessandra. Positioned on the sofa, Alessandra faced him with her arms crossed. She had to get this off her chest.

Romeo put down his glass, turned on the living room light and sat near her on the chair with his lips pursed. He scrutinised her as if he had something to say but was holding back. He peered past her. "What is it?"

Alessandra swallowed and gazed into her lap. "I apologise for calling you arrogant the other day when I barely know you." She couldn't explain how controlling he'd been with her, but she still had no right to prejudge him. "I don't want that to affect our working relationship."

He crossed his arms, nodding. "Apology accepted."

She rested back against the couch, her stomach tightening at the sound of his cold tone. "I need to check in with my friend, Mimi, and then my family. It's a decent time to call them now."

He held a neutral expression. "Sure. I will talk to you tomorrow."

Walking back to her bedroom, she set her laptop on the desk, signed into the video chat, and dialled in. She just partially closed the door behind her when her brother, Gianni, answered. "Hey, sis. How's it all going?"

"Good. How are you all doing? Missing me much?"

Gianni had shoulder-length brown hair, robust, soul-searching, dark eyes, and a tanned complexion. He was handsome and usually had no problems finding girlfriends. He was a few years younger than her but he normally acted like her father figure. "Not really. At least I can throw a word in with Dad now that you're not here."

"Ha ha, funny, funny. Where is Dad?" He rose and called out to him, and a minute later, he joined her on the call.

Her father, Dario, had kind, hazel eyes, a long chin, and black crew cut as if he was ready to serve in the army. Well into his fifties, he was still handsome for his age and she knew he had a girlfriend he was serious about. "Lessi, darling. How are you? I am missing you so much. When are you coming home?"

She chuckled. "Oh, Dad! I've only just started. Not for at least the next four to six months, depending on how quick they progress with the home." Footsteps sounded behind her, and she turned to see Romeo heading back to the kitchen. Oh, no. She knew she should have shut the door fully earlier.

Gianni came back on the screen. "Who was that, and why are you with a guy there? I assumed you had your own place."

"Ssh. Calm down." She rose and shut the door behind her, making sure that Romeo couldn't hear anything. "He is my colleague and he sleeps in a separate room. Not that you're my keeper, Gianni."

"He seems like a decent young gentleman, Lessi. What's his name?" her father asked.

Alessandra shook her head, not wishing to talk about a man she realised was controlling and yet found strangely attractive. She wouldn't be taken in by his appeal. "Romeo, Dad." She sighed. "And he is my colleague. He is..." She stopped short just in case he overheard their conversation. "Can we move on to other things, please."

Gianni inched forward. "Why are you blushing? Please don't tell me you're attracted to the guy. You understand you shouldn't be mixing work with pleasure, Alessandra. Maybe you shouldn't have taken this project on. It's too long on your own."

"This is an amazing experience for me, Gianni. It will give me a lot of exposure and credibility, and the villa will be spectacular once it's finished. It's going to have five bedrooms and a nearby cottage and is designed for entertaining."

"It sounds like a man with money to splash around," said her father. "As long as you get the recognition, Lessi. Remember, you are smart, talented, beautiful, and worthy of having a special man in your life who has heart and integrity."

Alessandra wished she could believe his words. "Thanks, Dad, but I'll be fine."

"Hmm," said Gianni. "Are there any women working with you?"

"No, they're all men, but they treat me well." If only Romeo saw her as an equal.

Gianni grimaced. "Is this Romeo treating you well, sis?"

"It's fine, Gianni. I can look after myself. Anyway, I need to go to sleep. Your afternoon is my night, so it is past my bedtime." She decided against calling Mimi for tonight. It could wait.

"Sure, sis. Have a great night and we'll talk soon. Love you."

"Love you too, Gianni. Bye, Dad."

He appeared concerned. "Lessi, I love you and make sure you enjoy yourself too. All work and no play makes it dull, but spend time with people who love and respect you. Goodnight."

She ended the call and undressed, preparing for sleep, knowing that Romeo was right next door. Did he sleep with pyjamas or not? Shaking away the erotic notions, she put on her summer nightwear, consisting of silky peach shorts and a low-cut matching top with short sleeves and a loose neckline.

Opening the door to her room, she entered the bathroom and brushed her teeth. A minute later, Romeo swept in as if he owned the place. But the expression on his face told her he didn't realise she was in the bathroom.

Hot damn! His body responded at the way her short shorts curved around her body from the back, and how her bare arms were slender and well-toned. When she turned around, he couldn't help but notice her low neckline and was curious about the curve of her breasts. She blushed and was gazing at him too. Even her floral scent made his heart race. *Stop it!* It was obviously the place that made him a little crazy. Being in a romantic place like Tuscany gave him illusions, and he was missing the company of a woman. That was all this was. He wasn't noticing her full lips or the way her fringe touched the corner of her eye. Her diamond-shaped brown eyes glanced at him so innocently. But he doubted she was innocent. Had she apologised to him earlier to get him on side before sweeping in and taking control of the work?

"I did not realise you were in here. I will come back." He rushed out of there before he lost his nerve.

Behind him, she said, "Fine."

He rested on his bed and put his arms over his head, trying to push away the image of her in the flimsy nightwear. Why would she put on such a thing when she was staying with him? It was hardly appropriate nightwear when a man was around. Any man would look, wouldn't they? It wasn't like he was attracted to her. Far from it.

When he heard footsteps, he assumed she was finished and headed back into the bathroom. It was going to be a long night. He was too wired to sleep now.

Chapter 8

SUPPLIES

"What do you mean, Mike can't make it?" asked Alessandra. "He's the carpenter and needs to make the decision here. We need to arrange it so we can move on to the next phase."

Romeo took a deep breath. "One of the guys made a mistake and Mike needs to make sure he fixes it. We can bring in samples and put in the order in the next day or so."

Alessandra's shoulders deflated, not sure she needed to spend more time than necessary with Romeo. "Fine. I guess we need to start considering flooring and I have ideas. I could use a few more samples."

He rubbed his hands together. "Okay. Let's go. It's a long drive to the building supply store."

As she got into the passenger seat, she pushed down her dress that fell above her knees. She spotted Romeo taking a quick peek at her legs, but it was crazy. It wasn't as if he saw her as attractive. Not even close "Where is this place exactly?"

"Almost an hour from here. A friend of Giuseppe's owns a building supply store, and we've used him before. He gives us good deals in timber."

She nodded. "How many projects have you had in Italy?"

"Twice before. Once in Montelpuciano and once in Florence. I can never seem to get enough of Italy and keep coming back."

"Would you prefer living here than Melbourne?"

He looked straight ahead. "I would miss my family living here, but I would most likely consider long-term jobs in Italy."

Heady with the scents of sandalwood and apple, Romeo must have been drowning in his cologne. His taut muscles rippled as he gripped the steering wheel and made turns around the hilly slopes, his shirt sleeves rolled up to his biceps. Even the trendy torn jeans, ripped at the knees, hugged his body well. "Where do you live back home?"

"My family is from Reservoir but I live in Preston. I didn't want to be too far from my two sisters and mother."

"And your father?"

He stiffened. "I would rather not talk about him."

Alessandra had seemingly hit a nerve, and she peered out at the passing vineyards, olive oil shops, and multitude of wine shops and bars. The medieval buildings in the distance captured her heart and she was in awe of the hilly, green terrain.

Romeo parked at the kerb and walked to an old building, stopping to wait for Alessandra . She joined him inside the store, and he waved to a man he knew. "Felice, how are you?"

The burly man of about sixty shook his hand firmly. "Fantastic. And who do you have here, Romeo?"

He turned to Alessandra. "This is Alessandra, the interior designer working with me on the commission. She's here to help make a few selections."

He nodded. "A pleasure to meet you, Alessandra. Are you Italian?"

"Nice to meet you too, and yes, I am Italian-born but now live in Carlton , Australia. I do miss this place, but I am grateful to be working in such a picturesque town. And I..." she stopped talking on realising Romeo's frustration. He seemed to be in a hurry to browse.

"Come on in and make your selections. I will give you time, then I will give you some off-cut samples for you to consider." He turned to Romeo. "How are Mike and Giuseppe?"

"They're keeping busy. Hard at work so they couldn't join me today."

As they browsed the building store, Alessandra took photos for reference. She slid her hands over the timber and pictured how it would fit into the space in her mind. Romeo passed her and was a few metres ahead when he waved for her to join him. "I like this terracotta and patterned tile. It's durable and practical. What are your thoughts?"

She shook her head. "No, I don't like it. Timber's the way to go." She took a few photos of timber samples with her phone. "I like these ones: the Baltic, slate, and granite. The hardwood's durable, and with a mixture of brown shades, it will soften harsh, colder colours and features and give it the rustic ambience we need. I'm sure Flavio will go with the timber rather than the terracotta."

He knit his brows. "I am taking note of this one and we will talk to Giuseppe about it. But your selections are fine too. Let's go with all four types. And possibly the matte rather than glossy surface."

Her heart warmed at his openness to her choices. "The matte's perfect. Sure."

They were back in the car, driving to a fabric store nearby. Romeo pulled up in front of the store and turned to her. "I'll wait in the car while you choose your samples."

She nodded and exited the car, swaying her hips in her short cotton dress. He had to admit she knew her work and had good ideas. If only they could agree on things.

He had heard part of her conversation with her family last night and knew that they had been talking about him. He wondered what she had said about him and whether she called him arrogant again. He was not arrogant simply because he had strong opinions and liked to work diligently.

His phone buzzed. Reaching for it in his back pocket, he answered a face time call and beamed at his sister, Adriana. "Hello there. This is a surprise."

Her long, black, glossy hair and grey eyes filled the screen. "Hey, bro. How's the gorgeous interior designer you're working with?"

He sighed and shook his head. "What makes you believe..."

"She's gorgeous. I checked her out on the Internet and I shudder to think how you're treating her. Not being too practical, are you?"

He loved his sister's quirky personality and would do anything for her after the way their father treated them, but she could be infuriating at the best of times. "I am doing my job and she is doing hers. We both do similar jobs, sis."

"Hmm. And are you getting along?"

He hesitated, not needing to give too much away. "Fine. How's Mum and Anne?"

"They're good, but Mum's needed a higher dose of her antidepressant meds, especially since you moved back to Italy. She misses you. But I don't want you to worry. She's in good hands and has her group of friends here. But don't change the subject. We were talking about you and Alessandra."

He pursed his lips. "There is no me and Alessandra. She is a colleague. If you must know, she had the nerve to call me arrogant. Of all things."

"Oh, bro. I am not surprised, but it's time you let go of the past and move on. Not all women are like your ex-girlfriend. From what I've read, she seems lovely, and if I got to know her, we'd be friends."

He sighed. "You have enough friends, Adriana." He peered through his window and spotted Alessandra exiting the store. Quickly, he made his excuses. "I have to go now."

"What? Not yet. I have more to ask you."

"Sorry, Adriana. Talk to you soon. I love you." He quickly ended the call as Alessandra placed two plastic bags on the back seat.

She sat in her seat and buckled up. "Sorry, I didn't mean to interrupt your call."

"It was only my sister checking in." Why did he tell her that? He had said too much. Sharing personal things with her was not what he intended.

Alessandra nodded. "Any chance we can go to the craft market to source a few more materials for my design model?"

He dropped his shoulders, grateful that she had asked nothing more about his family.

Chapter 9

DANCE MOVES

Alessandra sat back against the chair in the kitchen of the apartment a week later, sketching the last part of her design on her pad. She added in measurements then transferred the remainder of the design into her software on her laptop. Music from her phone played in the background.

Romeo was at the building site sourcing more materials. He was waiting on the delivery of the timber for flooring. She was thankful she had time for herself. Even better would be if she didn't meet with him at all today.

Once she finished the design on the computer, she moved to the living room and lingered near the coffee table. On it rested her design model of a miniature villa with the samples of flooring material, the fabric for window furnishings, and the miniature fireplace. Some of the samples she'd had in her suitcase but others she sourced at the craft shop when she had gone to the timber yard with Romeo a week ago.

She took a break and leaned into the cushioned comfort of the couch, listening to music from her playlist on her phone. She had been in Italy for only two weeks and over that time had accomplished a fair amount. The villa was coming along beautifully, and they were working on plastering today. At least the walls were going up. Each step brought them closer to her taking over.

In the last two weeks, she had become more familiar with Romeo, but still didn't trust his volatile and controlling persona. It was as if he couldn't relax for one day with all his rules of law. He was most likely allergic to fun. But despite his commanding presence, she had never truly asserted herself with him. Part of her held back, realising the ramifications of talking when it wasn't the right time. She had paid the price too many times when she had asserted herself with ex-boyfriends.

Alessandra rose from the couch, stretching out and slowly moving to the rhythm of Diamonds by Sam Smith. Flailing her arms and swaying her hips, she moved to the soft beats of the song, allowing it to permeate her soul as she shut her eyes and soared with the vibrations of the drums, voice, and tone of the music. *The Fighter* by Keith Urban and Carrie Underwood played next. She sang in tune with the song and danced to her heart's content, letting go of all her current personal challenges and pain of the past. Her feet tapped, her hands clapped, her voice spoke with the lyrics, and her upper body swayed from side to side. Surrendering, she let the music carry her into another world, a world of utopia without her hang-ups of men, of her mother, of Romeo.

Someone breathed heavily. She turned in shock horror at Romeo's cheeky grin. Shoulders deflating, she averted her eyes. "I didn't think you'd be back so soon," she said.

"Well, that was obvious."

"What were you doing?" Romeo asked.

"I was working on my design model and added my sketch to CAD. It's coming along well. And I considered a range of window furnishings and then for the cabinets, I thought of—"

Romeo put up his hand. "Stop and take a breather for a second." He sat beside her on the couch. *Christ!* The way her body knew how to move to the beats. The way he had a strong yearning to wrap his arms around her and join her in the dance. The way her full, rosy lips sang in tune to the music as if she'd had a singing lesson or two. Even the way the fabric of her dress lifted to show her feminine curves and tanned legs, going on for miles. Why was he affected by her escape, her joy for music? It had to be the heat making him crazy and delusional, easily affected by anyone dancing beautifully. "I didn't realise you liked to dance."

She kept her head straight, avoiding his eyes, the bottom part of her neck flushed. "I wouldn't call it dancing. It's only some fun. You should try it sometime."

He frowned. "I have fun when the time calls for it." When she kept silent, he carried on. "Can I have a gander at your playlist? I like Sam Smith, and I don't mind the old song by Keith Urban too."

She moved closer towards him, making him keenly aware of the soft tone of her knees and the silky smooth skin of her bare calves. She handed over her phone and he scrolled through her music. "It seems as though you like my music," she said.

"I do actually. I like The Weeknd, Bebe Rehxha, Dua Lipa, and Bruno Mars." He turned to her. "I wasn't expecting you to dance, and you can sing too."

She slowly turned in his direction. "I had a few singing lessons when I was in primary school, and part of it helped when..." Clearing her throat, she said, "Never mind. I'd better go back to work. Do you need me at the site?"

He shook his head. "No, it's fine. It seems as though you got a fair bit done here so take a break for today. We can get back to it tomorrow." Part of him wanted to stay sprawled on the sofa listening to her. It wouldn't hurt to find out what made her tick. He had noticed a vulnerability in her dance, as if she was fighting her own demons. But he might have been imagining that. She had been about to say something earlier but had stopped herself, and he didn't want to pry. Her issues were none of his concern as he had his own to deal with.

Romeo wasn't surprised that she'd had singing lessons as her voice sounded angelic yet strong. But he was focusing towards the end of the project. Then he wouldn't have to worry about Alessandra. He could go back to his life and she could go back to hers.

"I'm going for a power walk. I'll be back later," said Alessandra.

Romeo nodded. "Sure." He considered joining her, as a walk sounded like a good idea, but it seemed as if she wanted to avoid him and have her own space.

Chapter 10

MEMORIES

Inside the caravan, Alessandra leaned forward in her seat and pointed to her model while Romeo, Giuseppe, and Mike looked on. "This is the fully equipped kitchen and the timbers I've selected for the cabinets." She handed Giuseppe an A4 sheet of paper with a list of material selections. "This explains the ranges of timber for flooring, the fabrics and styles for window furnishing, and the painting samples for the walls in each room." Romeo scrutinised her model with a tilt of his head then pressed a finger across his lip. Those lips had her momentarily distracted until she regained control. "The first level will complement the ground level. I have a list of lighting fixtures to show Flavio. Once I have his approval, I can start ordering the materials in stages."

Mike nodded with a gleam in his eye. "This is amazing, Alessandra. Such detail." He turned to Romeo. "What do you think, big man?"

Romeo pressed his lips together. "Great. It appears that Flavio has a few decisions to make." His hands fidgeted as if he wanted to say something but held back. The intensity of his expression unnerved her.

"For wall displays, I have chosen a range of pieces by famous artists Flavio might be interested in, but he can decide on that later. There is obviously no rush on that. And I have suggestions for furniture for each room, downstairs to start with." She opened a magazine and pointed to dining tables, couches, and entertainment units.

Romeo put up his hand. "I think we need to slow down here and take one step at a time. How fast do you think the crew can complete the build? We are not even at the lock-up stage yet, so take a break, Alessandra."

She held her breath then exhaled, clenching her hands as she pasted on a fake smile. This was the way she worked. She got her concepts out there so they could discuss them. What didn't he grasp about this? He clearly didn't understand her process. Just because the villa wasn't ready didn't mean she had to be idle, not present her ideas and prepare materials ready to be ordered. How dare he ruin her process, her creativity? What did he know about interior design?

Giuseppe patted her gently on the shoulder. "Ignore the man. I love your ideas and the more you give me, the more I can take to Flavio. Leave this with me and I will speak to him. Great work, Alessandra."

Mike nodded. "This design model is stunning. Truly out there, young lady."

"Thank you. I'm glad you both understand my process." She avoided Romeo's eyes but she heard him sigh.

Giuseppe guided Alessandra by the arm to the door, casting a sharp glare at Romeo. "Let's go check the site and talk about some of your concepts. Romeo can brood here in the caravan if he likes."

Stealing a glance behind her, Romeo glanced into his hands and made no move as all three of them exited the caravan. Glad to have her space from him, Alessandra focused on Giuseppe leading the way.

Outside Mike's apartment, the team quietly considered the hilly view of Montepulciano. In the air clung the aromas of cut grass, fresh lemons, and white blossoms.

Romeo sat as far away from Alessandra as the table allowed while Mike took a seat at her right.

The steel of the chair cut into her lower back, so she shifted slightly. As she sipped on a glass of Lambrusco, the wind tossed her hair into her eyes. She drew it away from her face, ignoring the searing look coming from Romeo. What was he thinking? She wondered if he regretted talking to her rudely earlier this morning.

Mike drank down his beer and turned to Alessandra. "Romeo tells me you were born in Pisa. You must be glad to be back here for work?"

Alessandra turned to Mike. "It's good to be back. I love it here. Sometimes I wish I could have come sooner. I might visit Pisa for a few days afterwards."

Mike moved closer and briefly tapped her arm. "I, for one, am glad you're working with us. And I might even come and join you afterwards. I've always yearned to go to Pisa."

Romeo cleared his throat, glaring at Mike. "How about you go bring me a refill of beer?" He shifted his weight on the chair as if uncomfortable.

"Sure, man. Give me a sec." When Mike left, Romeo watched her in silence.

Alessandra broke the ice between them. "How long have you been friends with Mike?"

Romeo shrugged. "Since we were in primary school. We're more like brothers, but sometimes he can be full-on, so if you are uncomfortable in any way, tell him. Were you?"

Alessandra played dumb. "Was I what?"

"Uncomfortable."

Mike returned, and underneath his left arm, he held a photo album. Mike flipped open the album and positioned it next to Alessandra. "These are photos of Romeo and me when we were young. Check them out."

Alessandra glanced over at Romeo, whose face reddened. He shook his head while she scrutinised the photos: Romeo and Mike playing football together, playing on swings, licking an ice cream, and having dinner as a family. "Who are these here?"

Mike pointed and inched forward, shifting his body nearer to Alessandra. "These are my parents, my sister, Romeo's two sisters, and his father."

She turned the page and came across Romeo's father again, but this time, he stood next to Romeo in the kitchen with his arm lifted and his hand facing him as if he was about to strike him. "What's going on here?"

Mike winced. "Oh, sorry. I forgot that got in there. Just a joke, that is all." Before he could continue, Romeo rose from the table and knocked his chair to the ground.

Alessandra spotted him leave in a huff. "Is he all right?"

Mike frowned. "I am so stupid." He shook his head. "That photo shouldn't have been in there, and I'm a louse. Let me fix this." He got up and raced after his friend. Five minutes later, Mike returned. Sitting in his seat, he peered at her strangely. "He left and said to apologise to you. He asked if I could drive you back to your apartment. I'm sorry,

Alessandra, but he can be triggered like this sometimes. I wish he could get over his past, but he can't seem to. Stubborn old, mule."

"What happened to him?"

Mike clasped his hands and peered straight ahead, the breeze brushing over his messy hair strands. "I don't want to say too much as he'd have a fit, but all I can say is that his father was a piece of work. Always physically and emotionally abusing him until his mother left his father when he was a teenager. But..."

"The damage had already been done," she finished. Her stomach clenched tight as she imagined a younger version of Romeo in pain. Was that why he'd become hard and detached? Had he kept a shell as a veneer to protect himself from further pain?

Mike took deep breaths. "Exactly. Part of me hopes to sensitise him to all that stuff. You know?" He turned to her with a reassuring grin. "I think he likes you, but he needs to get over his past before he can learn to trust again. He's got a few good friends who have stuck by him all these years, but he struggles with female relationships."

Alessandra and Mike eventually turned to other subjects, but her mind wasn't fully focused on the conversation. Would Romeo ever open up to her about his past? Maybe if she shared something about herself, he might feel more comfortable. It was worth a try. But, then again, why was she so concerned whether Romeo opened up to her or not? Once this job was done, they'd be going their separate ways.

Chapter 11

DINING IN STYLE

R omeo walked into the Montelpuciano eatery, admiring the multi-coloured brickwork on the archway leading to vintage-style chairs and plank wood tables. Shelves of assorted wine bottles stood on their own in a climate-controlled space. Suspended light fittings consisted of black circular lamp holders with hexagonal patterns holding the pendant fixtures together, appearing sleek.

He appreciated the classical elements with the domes and arches adapted to contemporary purposes, with an ivory wall featuring brick wall paper, murals of old and popular Italian celebrities, giving it history with its rustic décor, chrome pipes on the ceiling and earthy colours.

Napkins inserted into glasses and people shuffling to their seats kept the waiters busy. He knew this eatery to be a symbol of Italian culture with its love of their range of pasta, assorted wines, followed by their espresso and caffe latte to be shared with a sweet pasty or cornetto, especially for breakfast.

The restaurant was unfamiliar to Romeo, but Flavio had insisted on meeting them here. Earlier in the day, Flavio visited the building site to check up on them. Cackling at Mike's jokes, Flavio appreciated the work so far. After viewing the samples Alessandra had prepared, Flavio was enthusiastic over her models and plans for the interior. Soon Flavio would arrive. No doubt he would be recognised and they would share an interrupted lunch, but whatever made their client happy was fine with Romeo.

Appearing nervous, Alessandra scanned their surroundings as they found a seat near the brick wall. Radiant in her revealing, red cotton dress and smooth olive skin, her lavender and soap smell inspired erotic notions he didn't welcome. Staunchly resisting his primal urges and failing, Romeo admired the way she nibbled her bottom lip and how she fingered her neck as she blushed. The way she averted her eyes from his glance, containing her anger, twisted his insides and set tension into his jaw. He would much prefer a screaming match to the quiet avoidance.

Part of him cringed at the way he had left Mike's place several days ago, but he couldn't cope with the images of his father. Despite the man being out of his life, the man continued to haunt him. Did Alessandra judge him and hate him for leaving her alone with Mike?

A loud voice behind him had Romeo twisting in his seat. "Alfonzo, darling. So great to see you again. I'm here to meet...Oh, there they are. Lead the way." The waiter nodded with a grin, then led Flavio to their table. His entourage remained outside.

Romeo stood and greeted Flavio with a handshake and Alessandra offered a meek wave.

"Nice to meet with you again, Alessandra." Flavio turned to Romeo. "I take it Giuseppe or the others aren't coming?"

"No, it's only the two of us," said Romeo.

Flavio sat to Alessandra's right, beaming at her as his gold bangles jingled over his wrists with every wave of his hands. His long, auburn hair was tied up in a low bun, and his coffee-brown eyes were vibrant and sharp. He was tall and solid in build.

He wore an oversized loose-sleeved floral t-shirt and tight-fitted white pants with wedged heels. His ears were adorned with dangly gold earrings and his eyes were marked with eyeliner. As a romance movie star, he transformed into an attractive heterosexual on screen, but, in reality, Flavio preferred male companionship. "Let's eat. I'm starving." He turned to the waiter who stood by their side. "Alfonzo, bring us the order I called in. Thanks."

The waiter was a stocky man with a missing tooth. "Certainly, Flavio. Anything for my favourite customer. Won't be too long."

Flavio faced Alessandra and held her hand. "I simply adore your ideas, darling. I will try to come back when you start on the furnishings, but it depends on my latest shoot. If we have more delays, I might not be able to make it."

"It's fine, Flavio. I understand you're busy." She beamed. "What's the movie about?"

Flavio turned briefly to Romeo. "A troubled man falls deeply in love with an equally traumatised woman, but they fight their feelings for several years. Then, one day, they bump into each other and decide to risk it. It was meant to be. Destiny."

Romeo huffed. "I don't believe in destiny, Flavio."

"I am inclined to disagree," said Flavio. "If true love is meant to be, the universe will make it happen and find a way to bring you back together. My destiny is about savouring different men in different countries, and I love it." He turned to Alessandra. "What about you? Is destiny your thing, girl?"

"I don't believe in destiny either. I believe it's about the choices we make that determine where we go in life. I don't know if we're meant to be with anyone, but who we decide on and not what the universe decides on."

The waiter interrupted their moment by setting down a platter filled with prosciutto, buffalo and mozzarella cheese, olives, bruschetta, and olive oil in a small, white dish. The aromas of hot bread, basil, and parsley permeated the air as the waiter brought a basket of homemade ciabatta bread. Romeo's mouth salivated as he dug in.

"This bread is delightful," said Romeo. He watched Alessandra's lips wrap around the bread after dipping it in olive oil and his body reacted. He swallowed with lust and imagined what it would be like to press those lips against his own. Italy and all this talk of romantic notions were playing with his mind.

Flavio nodded. "This is the best place in Tuscany, and I have planned something special for both of you." Romeo frowned. "I've arranged for both of you to take a winery tour first thing tomorrow. After the tour, you'll get to enjoy a nice lunch too. You guys deserve to be so pampered, and to let your hair down. My way of saying thank you, so far."

Romeo winced, not needing to spend alone time with Alessandra. "But why, Flavio? You're already paying us for your villa. This is not necessary." His hands fidgeted under the table, and he'd suddenly lost his appetite.

Flavio waved his hand and shoved an olive into his mouth. He picked up a piece of prosciutto and put it onto the bread then took a bite. "Oh, of course it is, darling. I don't need you guys to be all work and no play. The more you get to see Tuscany, the more creativity will flow. I want you to soak up this atmosphere. Now, I've mentioned the changes I would like in both of your designs, but to really capture the flavour of Montepulciano, you have to experience as much of this culture as possible."

"That is very generous of you, Flavio, but there really is no need. It is appreciated but it is too much," said Alessandra.

Romeo's chest constricted but he didn't know why. Did it bother him that Alessandra didn't want to go with him to this winery tour?

Flavio sighed with a shake of his head. "Oh, nonsense. Before things get even busier, now's your chance to take a breather. You'll have fun. I promise you, darlings. Enjoy!" He devoured the rest of his bread and winked at Alessandra. What was that about?

When the next lot of meals arrived, Romeo was mostly full but he could eat a little more Italian food. Fragrant herbs, smoky cheese, and tangy tomato sauces wafted through the air as the waiter set bowls of tagliatelle bolognaise, creamed gnocchi, and tomato-based agnolotti on to the table.

Alessandra plated up after he and Flavio served themselves. She chewed on gnocchi while intermittently watching Romeo. Something about the way she regarded him showed a hint of sadness in her eyes. A vulnerability. What was going through that brain of hers, and did he care to know? "This is to die for, Flavio. Great choices but how do you expect us to have dinner tonight? This will last me for a week."

Flavio dabbed at his t-shirt where cheesy sauce dripped. "Whatever is left here, I'll get Alfonzo to deliver it to your apartment. You can have it for dinner tomorrow night."

Romeo laughed at Flavio's sense of humour over the next hour until it was time to leave. "Thank you for lunch, Flavio."

Alessandra grinned as she walked to the exit of the restaurant. "You are too kind."

Flavio grabbed her hands and held them in his own. "Darling, if I wasn't part of the other team, I would marry you in a heartbeat. You are gorgeous, creative, smart, and have a beautiful heart, and I'm surprised no-one has married you yet." He gave Romeo a brief glance.

Romeo changed the subject. "Your next film project's here in Tuscany, isn't it?"

Flavio nodded. "It is, and I am sure the villa will be done before shooting starts." He grinned. "I must leave you now. A car will pick you up for your winery tomorrow morning at 10:30 a.m., so be ready by then." He flailed with his hand again. "I will not hear anything more about it. Just enjoy and soak it up." He kissed them both on the cheek and disappeared into the throng of people outside of the door.

Romeo hated that part of him looked forward to spending a day with Alessandra on the winery tour.

Chapter 12

WINERY TOUR

Alessandra slid into the back seat of the car while Romeo got into the passenger's seat. The driver was a burly man who barely spoke on the way to the winery in the heart of Montepulciano. Romeo's posture was stiff and he was quiet.

The short trip led them to the historical square's stone buildings near an arched doorway where a group of ten others waited. Alessandra stepped along the gravel path, the warmth enveloping her. The gentle wind grazed her cheeks as she made her way past an eatery, the loud voices and laughter of people bringing her to attention. Smells of strong coffee, nutmeg, and cinnamon permeated her senses. White umbrellas over round tables fluttered. She touched a stone fountain beneath a group of animal statues, and flinched at the heat of the sun's rays on its surface. Pulling out her phone, she snapped a few pictures of the surrounding area while Romeo put his hands in the pockets of his shorts, turning his head in all directions.

After ten minutes of waiting, he lifted his arm to peer at his watch. "Where is that guide? He's late."

He truly was a stickler for rules "Relax, Romeo. We don't have to be on a schedule." She ignored his extended attention on her bare legs.

The heat stifled her even in her white cotton dress and she fanned herself, standing awkwardly next to Romeo, who stared at two children running around playing tag while the adults next to them yelled in their direction.

Rare clouds dotted the blue sky. Stretching into the distance, green huddled trees lined hilly slopes and extensive vineyards. The woody perfume of fern, pine, and chestnut trees reminded her of family trips she took as a child around Pisa before her mother left them. The vineyard made her nostalgic, bringing to mind long-forgotten childhood memories. Sharp scents of oak, sweet spices, and delicate florals mingled with bitter and pungent olives and cheeses to be served along the tour.

The young tour guide arrived ten minutes later sporting khaki pants and a floral shirt. Absentmindedly, he scratched his stubble. After ticking off names, he scanned the group. "Welcome to the winery tour. You will be amazed by the activities here today. My name is Gianni and I'll be your guide and local sommelier. First off, we will visit a historic cellar that dates back to the sixteenth century and we'll learn about the assorted wines made on this vineyard." He rubbed his hands together. "Then you will sample some of the finest wines with Tuscan appetisers and a hearty lunch. Let's move, people." He raced inside and the group followed him into a refreshingly cool underground cellar with arched ceilings and smooth flooring.

Colossal barrels rested in rows on either side of the group. Long planks of wood supported each barrel. "Here we have a range of wines; the rosso di Montepulciano DOCG and the Nobile di Montepulciano DOCG. The DOCG means we have the strictest of guidelines when making our wine. It is the Italian system of labelling and protecting our fine Italian wine, in the legal sense. Those with the DOCG status need to pass a detailed lab analysis with a panel of tasters to ensure the high standard of the wine. The DOCG status makes it the highest quality wine. The Montepulciano grape is widely grown around parts of Central Italy, mainly in Abruzzo, Marche, and Molise areas. This type of grape makes dry red wines. Any questions so far?"

Alessandra switched off when a few people asked questions, glancing at Romeo who had neared one of the barrels and rested his hand on it. Romeo focused on the guide, but she couldn't stop staring at the way his blue shorts fit around his tanned, muscled legs, while his tight fitted white t-shirt showed off every dip and line of his chest and abs. *Get a grip! Stop this!*

Moving along to another area, the new tunnel featured a private collection of wine bottles where

Gianni gave them a spiel of their methods and processes for making the wine. She did her best to focus on the talk.

The air in the converted Etruscan tomb was heady with wine must and earth, reminding her of a trip she had taken to a wine cellar in Pisa as a child. She noticed that the tomb was carved out of natural, solid rock, as Gianni had mentioned, as she continued to listen to the history of the cellar's underground space with its vaults and tunnels, heavily influenced by Etruscan civilisation,.

Gianni rambled on. "Other important buildings include Palazzo di Bucelli, featuring a foundation built of carved Etruscan burial urns full of cement and stacked like bricks. These urns have Etruscan and Latin inscriptions."

The group huddled close together. Alessandra winced at the tight space, almost bumping into a rack of wine bottles as she squeezed through the arched walkway with its minimal lighting and flat ground.

One of the young children bumped into Alessandra, knocking her into Romeo. Catching her waist, he steadied her. His hands warmed her body as he locked eyes with hers. "I am so sorry," said Romeo.

His green eyes softened, and she noticed the faint stubble around his upper lip. She lingered on his protruding biceps, flexed from his grasp around her waist. His expression hinted at concern.

Their faces were within inches of one another's. Alessandra immediately broke eye contact, her heart beating fast and mouth dry. She was startled by the voice of a young woman. "I am so sorry. They get bored."

She turned to the group who were way ahead as the young woman shook her head in the direction of the child who had his head bowed.

"It's fine," said Alessandra who refocused on the guide in the near-distance. Romeo turned away, scanning the exit to the tomb. She had to get a grip on herself.

Chapter 13

CURIOSITY

Their next stop was the outdoor vineyard, and Gianni explained the harvest and what types of wines used a particular type of grape. The hot breeze brushed her face as she wandered behind Romeo who focused on the guide.

Finally, they were led to the tasting courtyard. Alessandra stood at a table with assorted wines, unsure of where to start.

Romeo picked up two glasses and handed one to Alessandra. "You should like this one: the Burberosso. It's an intense taste and goes well with Pecorino cheese." He pointed to the tasty-looking cheeses and crackers on the table. Alessandra put a piece of cheese on a cracker and bit into it, savouring the blend of the wine and cheese. As she focused on her palate, she tasted berries, herbs, and a hint of coffee in the wine.

"You understand your wines, don't you?" said Alessandra.

Gianni spoke up again, brandishing a bottle. "This here is the Ombra white wine, which is fruity and spicy and has the flavours and aromas of Tuscany. Have it with the extra virgin olive oil on a slice of bread, and it's heavenly. A fine match." He poured a few glasses and Alessandra tried the white wine then a slice of bread dipped in olive oil. The strong olive taste and soft texture of the bread melted in her mouth, and her palate wanted more. The wine was dry yet refreshing.

After trying several more wines with Gianni's detailed descriptions, he whisked them through glass sliding doors that led them to a dining area, which featured brick flooring and square tables surrounded by hard-backed timber chairs. "Lunch is served. Thank you for coming and have fun with the rest of your day." He rushed off, no doubt having another tour to complete.

Plates of ham, a range of cheeses, bread, dip, savoury biscuits, prosciutto, and black olives lined the table with a bottle of wine. Romeo and Alessandra took a seat and poured themselves the red Burberosso wine.

Alessandra chewed on bread and considered the others in the group delving into their lunch. "It was interesting. I love learning about wines."

Romeo nodded. "Me too. I've been on a few of these Tuscan wine tours and I never get tired of their different but similar processes." He shifted. "It's amazing how depending on the ingredients, two of the same wines can be completely different. It only takes a little change to make a huge impact on the flavour."

She nodded. "That's true. They all have their precise recipes and measurements to get it just right. Do you prefer dry or sweet?"

He held his glass. "Definitely dry, but I'm guessing you prefer the sweet variety?"

Alessandra beamed. "You guessed correctly." She popped an olive into her mouth, tasting the salty yet soft texture. "I love wineries and the natural landscape of it all. It's the slow, savouring pace of the country vineyards, and the colourful views from the distance. I like mainly the red wines which to me taste richer and a bit heavier than the white wines. I always loved the landscape of wineries when I lived here. When I was just a child, my parents believed that if they exposed me to wine at a young age, I'd become an alcoholic. Their forbidding made it so much more interesting to me."

Romeo laughed. "It seems like they were protective of you."

"One more than the other." She turned away, not wishing to discuss her mother when she'd had such a pleasant time on this tour. "It was generous of Flavio to do this for us. He's an amazing guy and seems to get so much joy out of life." She dipped her bread into a basil and olive dip and took a bite.

"He is a man who has achieved so much and deserves all the riches he has. He's got a great mind for business and money and is quite ambitious. I respect him for it." He lifted his posture. "Do you have any ambitions, Alessandra?"

She nodded. "I...I hope to start my own business, and this project will hopefully help."

He fixated on her. "Right. What type of business? Interior design?"

She was seeing a different side to Romeo, but she didn't know why it unnerved her a little. "I love interior design because I want more freedom to choose the clientele and businesses to work with. I like to be flexible, and in this way I can set my own hours."

"You have talent, Alessandra, and I am sorry I've been hard on you. I am sure you can make that happen with the experience you'll get on this villa. This is a huge project and the exposure you'll get will make people notice. We all have dreams."

She was curious about his dreams, but would he share them with her? "What are your dreams, Romeo?"

Romeo rested against the hard-backed chair, watching her curiously. He yearned to know what triggered that dark, vulnerable abyss in her expression. "I plan to build a drop-in-centre for youths back in Melbourne. It's something I always aspired to do to help those with mental illness."

Alessandra inched forward as she sipped her wine, her eyes darting around the dining area. "Amazing goal. What made you decide on that?"

He rested back against his chair. "My mother had mental health problems, and I'd like to help others like her. Mental illness is so widespread in the world, and I'd like to do my share." He shifted topic. "Flavio has a vested interest in the mental health centre and plans to fund it, provided he's satisfied with the villa."

She nodded. "That is amazing news about Flavio, and I am sorry about your mother. Mental illness is a huge issue these days, but at least it's less stigmatised now. Even with government funding and mental health care plans, they only scratch the surface for therapy. It's never enough."

"Thanks, and yes, the funding is never enough. I plan to organise unlimited therapy in the drop-in centre so people get as much help as they need. Not only for treatment but for maintenance therapy."

She angled her head. "Great idea. It's a huge contribution you're making."

Romeo pursed his lips. "It might sound better in theory than in practice. We'll have to wait and see."

She squared her shoulders. "You can only try it out but talking therapy's not for everyone. I prefer the creative therapies."

He nodded. "Talking can sometimes be over-rated. I prefer results through my actions." He placed a finger under his chin, curious about her creative side. He remembered walking in on her dance. "Tell me more about your love of dance."

She blushed. "I had a passion for dance when I was about nine but it soon died. I no longer had the motivation or interest in Australia." She frowned. "Now, I'm discovering that dance is a great way for me to express myself. My joys and my pain. I like to dance for the pure fun of it." She averted her eyes, the base of her throat turning red.

"I noticed you have a natural talent for it. Did you have lessons?"

"I did, but later I lost interest—too much going on and family issues. I had lessons in Italy for about a year until moving to Melbourne. I stopped and a part of me regretted it, but all things come to an end eventually." She peered into her lap and her upper body hunched over her glass. "Tell me about why you became an architect."

He swallowed. "My sister's toy dollhouse broke once, and I promised her I would fix it. I experimented with materials using ice cream sticks and felt fabric. I liked the way it gave me control over something, being able to mould something from nothing. It was when I decided it would be my life-long career."

He questioned why he revealed that. It must have been something in the wine that made her easy to talk to today.

Chapter 14

A RELEASE

The next morning, Alessandra accepted a video call on her laptop as she was drinking a cup of coffee. It was her friend, Mimi. Searching, she didn't see or hear Romeo anywhere and assumed he was either still asleep or had gone for his daily jog. Crazy to run in this heat.

"Hey, Mia. How are things, girl?"

Her slender frame filled the screen and she tilted her head. "I saw your social media pages about the job, and wow…He is absolutely gorgeous, Alessandra. That man, Romeo, you are working with."

She shuddered. "Hmm. If you say so. I hadn't realised." She finished off the last remnants of coffee and put the mug into the sink. "Can you wait a minute?" Her friend nodded. Inside her bedroom, she shut the door and resumed her conversation.

"And how's work in the hospital going?"

"Good, but no hot men where I work. Don't change the subject. I am sure something is going on between you two. The photos of Romeo on his social media pages blew my mind. He is that hot. You'd make a gorgeous couple and would look perfect together. I am sure there's something there. What's the story, hon?"

Alessandra pondered. *Couple? With Romeo? No way. Not another controlling man.* Besides, it wasn't like he was even the least bit interested in her, not at all. "Nothing, Mimi. We just work together and nothing else. No story there."

"Oh, come on. At least admit he's hot."

"Fine, he might be easy on the eyes, but I'm not interested. This is the biggest project I've worked on and have to keep my head in the game. I cannot fail Flavio."

"And you won't, but you need to take in the sights there too. Take a break. In that way, you can be more inspired and get those creative juices flowing."

"I have been relaxing. Just the other day, Flavio arranged for us to go on a winery tour, and it was amazing. You know how much I love wineries. The food was delicious and the wine high quality."

"Was it just you and lover boy or did the other workers go too?"

She scoffed. "Oh, come on, Mimi. Do not call him that. I can at least say we're becoming friendly. He might crack his aloof and hard veneer."

"It seems like you have a challenge on your hands. I say, bring it on, hon." Her friend's expression turned serious. "I worry about you, girl. Is he at least treating you well?"

Alessandra didn't need to get into it too much. She had to keep focused on the present. "He can be dominating, arrogant even, and he once mentioned I was inexperienced, which I admit I am. I haven't done such a big-scale project before and it is daunting. I am not sure if I can fulfil his expectations or Flavio's."

Mimi waved her hand in her direction. "Oh, stop it, hon. You have to treat yourself better. Do not let any man say you're not enough, because you are. You have impeccable interior design skills. You're smart, beautiful, a loyal friend, and you have resilience and heart, and do not, I repeat, do not let a man tell you otherwise, or they will have me to deal with. Just be assertive, girl. Don't let anyone put you down anymore. The past is done and you can grow from that experience."

"Thanks, Mimi. I hear you, but it's hard. This sense of not being good enough creeps up every now and then, and it's hard to shake. I wish I had your faith in me, but I'll work on it." She let the tears out, a mixture of pain and joy at having a friend who had always had her back.

"I am sure you will, hon. But those ex-boyfriends of yours who hurt you will never do that again. And whoever you choose next will be someone who respects you for you and doesn't need to mould you into something you're not."

Alessandra nodded. "I love you, girl. So much."

"I love you, too. If at any time you want to talk, message me. Take care of yourself and we'll speak soon."

"Bye, Mimi." She ended the call and shut the laptop, her mind reeling over the different voices in her head. *You're worthless, you won't amount to anything, you could do with a breast enhancement, and you're a stupid bitch.* No, she had to take those voices out of her head.

Romeo passed by Alessandra's door and heard voices inside her room. His gut clenched. She was crying, but he couldn't tell if they were tears of joy or sadness. But it hit him hard in the chest. Why did he even worry so much? Women cried all the time, and this was none of his concern. Needing a shower, he quietly shut the bathroom door behind him.

As he showered, he couldn't stop picturing her face stained with tears and wished them away. The sound of her crying reverberated in his ears, and he envisioned himself wrapping his arms around her, comforting her, reassuring her. Had she been through something traumatic? His hands tightened around the soap, inspired by his protective instincts, his head shaking at anyone who had caused her pain. Then thoughts of her poured through him: the way her hair flowed neatly around her shoulders, the way she shyly averted her gaze when nervous, the biting of her bottom lip when she was in deep thought, and the scrunching of her nose as she was working on her laptop.

He imagined her soft curves against him, remembering the cleavage in her nightgown and the way he had held her tightly around the waist in the wine cellar. Turning away from thoughts of her, she kept popping up into his mind and he felt himself go hard. Fantasy overtook him, forcing arousal through him violently. His hand had felt so good against her waist, her breasts looked so soft and inviting. Thoughts of her naked, his hands trailing over her, made him painfully hard. If he didn't release himself now, he would go mad. Slick with moisture, he wrapped a hand around himself and squeezed.

Romeo had to bite back a moan of pleasure. He was so close already. What if she heard him? What if she caught him, here in the shower? That thought sent him over the edge and he pumped himself hard and fast. One. Two. "Alessandra..." he sighed, barely a whisper. Three. What would it feel like inside of her? Hot. Four. Squeeze. Heartbeat so strong he could feel it beneath his hand as he synchronised his pumps with it. Knees growing weak with his rising pleasure, Romeo braced a hand against the shower wall. Five. Six. Seven. Eight. Nine. Ten. The final stroke sent him over the edge, quivering with his release.

Cutting off the groan of frustration rising in his throat, Romeo cranked the water cold. It hadn't been enough. It hadn't even taken the edge off. Romeo still wanted her, and he wanted her bad. The cold shower helped, but just barely.

Once he exited the shower, he dressed, and headed to the kitchen for a light breakfast. Swinging open the fridge, he selected the bowl of fruit and set it on the table, his face warming when Alessandra walked towards him, Romeo turned away and filled a glass with tap water. "Good morning," he said. Peering over his glass as he sipped, he appraised her for any sign of pain or sadness. She seemed her usual vibrant self, but was that a mask to hide her true pain? He was clutching at straws. It would be wiser if he asked her, but now was not the time to dig into her mind. It was time to go to work.

She retrieved a bowl from the cupboard, picked up a few strawberries, washed them under the tap, and sat down. Picking up a strawberry, she wrapped her lips around it, the sight of her tongue making him hard again. He yearned to nuzzle her neck to get closer to her soap and perfume scent.

"The winery was interesting the other day," she said.

He nodded, focusing on something else other than her full, rosy, wet lips. Reciting schematics and measurements in his head, Romeo's lust gave way to logic, finally. Biting into a piece of honeydew, he sat beside her. "It was nice. I guess it's something we both have in common. Wine and wineries. It's the Italian in us that relishes a glass of rich wine with our meals and loves a good conversation."

She beamed. "It did remind me of my time here, and part of me misses living in this historical place. I wonder, sometimes, if my life would have taken a different turn if I grew up in Italy."

"Hmm. Aren't you happy with your life in Melbourne?"

Alessandra frowned, her eyes moving away from him momentarily, hesitating. "Sure." She smiled weakly and reached into her bowl for the final strawberry. Rising, she rinsed her bowl in the sink and put it on the dish rack. Turning to him, she said, "I'll brush my teeth and then I'll be ready to go."

"Of course. We'll leave soon." He watched her leave, that hint of vulnerability showing in her eyes again. He wanted to tap into that sadness behind her vibrant and bubbly personality, help her heal it, but would she share it with him?

Part of him craved to push away his growing attraction but another part of him wished to run with it.

Chapter 15

INSIGHT

Alessandra walked around the building site with a clipboard in hand as she scribbled notes. Standing near a plank of wood, she put down her clipboard and picked up her measuring tape from the ground. Romeo stood opposite her and held the other end of the tape as he shouted out the measurement. Writing it down, she said to Romeo, "We need more space for the couch with this wall here. The one I had in mind is too big for this area. It won't fit as it is. Can we make adjustments?"

Romeo sighed, gripping the blueprint so firmly he was wrinkling the edges. "Are you kidding me? We need to use my specifications. Adding more space means it shifts everything else. It will not work." He took a deep breath, clearly showing his exasperation.

She exhaled and clenched the clipboard in her fist. If her design fell short, she could miss her chance at developing a reputation as a designer in her own right. She could miss the opportunities to truly make a name for herself. It had to be the best design she could make it, and she didn't need Romeo thwarting her ambitions. Time to make a stand. "I am sorry, Romeo. I don't see how this change can shift much. Why can't we compromise here and look at the interior design that matches what Flavio wants? He liked this part of the design I showed him, and he likes that couch. It will not fit here with this wall that needs to be extended. Can't you make it work?"

Romeo swallowed, scrutinising the blueprint as he made his way around the site and let her wait for a response. "Listen. Why can't you alter your design space? Can't you pick another couch? Don't you think it's a lot easier than me having to remeasure these walls which impact the other rooms?" He pursed his lips and glared in her direction.

She swallowed and measured her words. "I need to make the living room the absolute best it can be, and this is what Flavio would like. It's got to be trendy, have flair, and keep up with modern times. This is the couch that works and the one Flavio insisted on."

He sighed. "It's your job to make the interior work with the existing structure of the home. I have busted my gut for days and nights on this, and not to have it changed simply because of your current whim, Alessandra."

She briefly turned away, her rage shaking the clipboard. Her throat dried up and her cheeks warmed. Averting her eyes, she turned away and scurried into the caravan, needing time to collect herself. Luckily, Romeo did not follow her. She couldn't be near him right now.

As soon as she reached the caravan, she sat at the table and bowed her head. She took deep breaths and considered ways to break the news to Flavio.

Romeo threw the blueprint on the ground and cursed. The nerve of that woman, believing that she didn't have to fit in with the planned structure. Did she think it was easy coming up with these specifications, slaving over the plan day and night, living on little sleep? Why was she taking control of his project? If his reputation wasn't stellar after this, he might as well kiss his drop-in centre goodbye. The deal with Flavio would fall through. He had to focus on his goal. People needed his centre as much as he needed to make a difference in the world. But then again, if this was the way Flavio envisioned the space with this couch, then shouldn't he be compromising?

Bile rose in his throat, and he lifted his face to the sky, at a loss as to what he should do next. He didn't want to confront Alessandra in the caravan, and he couldn't leave for the apartment or she'd be stranded here.

Giuseppe and Mike approached him, staring daggers. "What?" Romeo barked.

Mike shook his head with his hands on his hips. "Jesus, Romeo. We could hear you a mile away, yelling like two children fighting for the same candy bar. What gives?"

Giuseppe clapped him roughly on the shoulder. "I love you like my own son, Romeo. But the way you spoke to that poor young girl in there was downright rude. You need to apologise to her. Now."

"She needs to understand that it's harder for me to make changes than it is for her. I mean, how hard is it to choose a different couch?" Romeo focused on the pieces of plank stacked two metres away and kicked at a few screws lying on the ground.

Giuseppe exhaled. "This project is obviously important to both of you but she is trying to do her job too. Flavio agreed to that design and that couch, so why not compromise?" He inched forward. "You understand how fussy Flavio is, and he definitely loves that couch. I suggest you make it work. It's not going to make much of a difference."

Mike tapped him playfully on the cheek. "I love you, bro, but it's no way to treat Alessandra. She is not your cheating ex-fiancée or your father. You need to get over yourself and do the right thing. Stop trying to control every damn thing in your life. Embrace flexibility." He huffed. "I know you need more openness, like Alessandra. I suggest you apologise and tell her you'll fix it."

Romeo felt like he'd been slapped in the face, but they were right. He had been hard on her. She was a colleague and tried to do as good a job as he did. Would she forgive him?

Chapter 16

AN APOLOGY

R omeo cautiously opened the door and headed inside the caravan. Alessandra had her head down and was scribbling notes
on a pad while sorting through samples of fabric spread out over
the table. She briefly lifted her head and kept her focus on her pad,
scribbling more words he couldn't decipher. Her shoulders slouched
and her sad expression tugged at his heart. What could he say to make
things better?

He cleared his throat and tugged on the base of his neck as he sat
down across from her. Putting his elbows on the table, he picked
up a soft velvety fabric and rubbed it between his fingers. "I'm sorry
about...you know."

Alessandra scoffed. "No, I don't know. Why don't you tell me?"

He stared into her eyes, noticing the redness in them. Had she been
crying? Surely, he wasn't that bad with his words? "I was a bit harsh
with what I said. Can we move on and attempt to work together?"

She swallowed. "Of course. No problem. I am a big girl and can take
whatever you dish out." She pulled out her laptop from her bag and
set it on the table. "If you'll excuse me, Romeo. I have a design to work
on and Flavio to speak to."

He put up his hand. "Listen, I can make it work with the wall. There is no need to talk to Flavio. Order the couch. There might be a slight delay, but we can take a time out."

She pressed her lips together. "Thank you. I appreciate that." Frowning, she said, "Why were you so angry with me? You over-reacted out there."

He swallowed, wondering how much to tell her. "I might be a tad emotional with my work because I have set plans, and I need to maintain my reputation. If we have too many delays because of these changes, word gets around, and I won't be offered jobs here again. As I mentioned before, I have this deal with Flavio and if I don't do a perfect job on his villa, I won't secure the funding for it."

She nodded. "All the more reason to go with what he likes. But I do admire what you're doing and I can understand having those passions." Alessandra nibbled her bottom lip and closed her laptop. She picked it up and put it back inside her bag. "Right now, we need to go through the remainder of those rooms and come up with practical plans." She rose, retrieving her notepad and pen.

"Are you okay? You look like you were crying. I hate to think I hurt you..." Romeo said softly.

fell forward. Romeo pulled at her hands and steadied her in place. Their eyes locked, lingered. "I am fine, Romeo. I have to go." Leaving her bag inside the caravan, she pushed past him and hurried outside.

Romeo stood dumbstruck, his heart beating a mile a minute. He had hurt her, he realised. Kicking himself, he slammed a fist against the table with a loud bang. Damn his need for control. What was he going to do?

Alessandra steeled herself as she walked back to the site, nodding to a few contractors and smiling at Giuseppe and Mike who were drilling into a wooden frame inside the kitchen space. As she wandered through to the living room, she couldn't help but dwell. Did Romeo think he could solve everything by asking her to open up to him when he'd been rude to her earlier? It was such a lame apology. And what was with his knight in shining armour routine all of a sudden? He had been the one to hurt her and now he wanted to make it better because he felt guilty? Let him face his own guilt.

She focused on making notes on her designs, squeezing through a doorway. She imagined the adjusted wall and the couch Flavio liked resting back against it. When she walked back inside the space, she made new notes, drawing inspiration from the colour themes on her design model and the view of the mountainous terrain, picturing a plush rug underneath the couch, throw pillows in each corner of the sofa, and a low Baltic wood table levelled with it. She envisioned sliding doors leading out to the Tuscan countryside. She would design the space for the TV and a rustic-looking bar with counter space featuring cupboards and book stands, decorative knick knacks, and an ottoman nearby. She focused up high to jot down notes on lighting fixtures. Giuseppe appeared at her side.

"Can I check out your notes?" he asked.

"Sure," she said, happy to share her work with someone who supported her.

She handed the pages to him then spotted Romeo coming out of the caravan. Her stomach tightened at the way his jaw stiffened.

Giuseppe handed back her notepad. "I like your designs, but for these kinds of materials, you'll have more of a selection in Sienna or Florence. Given the distance, you might need to stay a few days. Why don't you and Romeo head over to those cities tomorrow so you can bring in samples and take photographs of what you like? I can book you a place to stay. It is about work and Flavio would definitely approve it."

She shuddered at the notion of being away with Romeo after the way he treated her. Was it such a great idea? Was it wise to be staying together in a hotel when she needed to keep her distance? But no, this was about work and they would no doubt be in separate rooms. "Okay then. You can talk to Romeo and get his perspective." She noticed Romeo talking to Mike. "If I can go through the rest of this area, we can accomplish a lot tomorrow. Then once we are sure about what we like, we'll show them to you." Taking a breath, she said. "My goodness! This project is huge and four months is a tight timeline."

He smiled. "Possibly, but we still have time. Flavio is aware of possible delays. Don't worry. We'll do our best to reach the deadline, but a lot of this is out of our control. A lot falls on these talented craftsmen over here." He waved his hands around. "Come on. Let's go over the rest here."

Alessandra walked alongside Giuseppe through the framed-up library area, sitting room, and the bar and billiards room while the subcontractors framed up one of the five bedrooms. By the end of the day, she was tired, hungry, and in need of a long sleep.

Chapter 17

A JOURNEY

The next day, Alessandra set down her travel bag in her hotel room next door to Romeo's. He had driven for an hour and a half to Florence, most of the time in silence.

The room had clean floorboards, and one of the grey walls displayed a painting of the local mountainous terrain. A double bed with its grey headboard blended into the wall, and a small table in the corner featured a desk lamp, electric kettle, and coffee cups. Beside it under the draped window was a padded chair, and a beige couch opposite a TV set.

Half an hour later she met with Romeo outside the hotel to take a walk to a local curtain shop. She brushed through the hanging curtains with Romeo beside her. "This beige blackout curtain would suit the living room. What do you think?"

Romeo squinted as he fingered the fabric. "Maybe." He walked past her and focused on a blind. "I like this double roller blind. It's peach. Flavio might prefer the pastel tones."

"Hmm. Possibly." She walked over to view it as it hung against the wall. "It can soften the living space, that's for sure." Her eyes darted around the area. "The pink drapes would match well with these white lace curtains." The texture of the fabric was soft with its intricate pattern. "This Roman blind would go well in the kitchen."

Romeo nodded. "I like all of them you mentioned except for the red drapes. Too bland, but it's up to Flavio. Show him the samples and he can decide." He pressed his lips together. "You know more about window furnishings than I do."

Was that an actual compliment, she wondered. Alessandra rummaged in her bag for her phone and took photos then collected samples of the selections they both admired to furnish the windows for the villa. "I do have experience with all kinds."

"I appreciate the way Flavio wants to blend the rustic style with a modern look. It gives a taste of both worlds."

As they walked outside the curtain shop, Romeo patted her gently on the shoulder. "I am sorry about yesterday. I didn't mean to overstep with..."

"It's forgotten, Romeo. Let's focus on our mission here."

Ambling down a narrow street, the sweltering air made the back of her neck sweat as she winced at the fumes, dust, and debris coming from passing cars.

"Hungry?" he asked.

She nodded. "I could eat."

Romeo led them inside a restaurant and they pushed through a crowd to a table. She turned to Romeo who sat next to her when a short, stout waiter approached to take their orders. About five tables too many were crammed into the dining area, making patrons brush shoulders or bump chairs together if they moved. Though the tones of conversations were hushed, the walls were so close that the soft words echoed and overlapped, creating a noise that congested the air.

After ordering their drinks and food, Alessandra looked around, the expression on Romeo's face having softened since their silent drive down here.

"I took a few photos, and hopefully, Flavio will like one of them at least. But I am glad he has agreed to most of my ideas so far." She sipped her water. "I have done this for the past six years, so I hope Flavio sees that reflecting in the samples I've chosen."

He knit his brows. "I can see how hard you work and I'm sure Flavio appreciates that." He chugged most of his beer. "What you do is different to my work, but my work is creative in parts too. As I said, I tend to be somewhat passionate with my work, and what you suggested with the door and the wall makes sense."

Alessandra laughed. "I know we started off poorly, but let's talk about something else." She downed more of her wine. "Tell me more about your mental health drop-in centre. Where do you plan to build it and how will it work?"

"I plan to renovate an old home I bought years ago. It's a small modern-style home and will need extensions and repairs. A huge feat. But with Flavio's funding, my architectural design, and a building permit, it should hopefully go ahead."

She nodded. "It's a good idea to change your old home into a centre."

The waiter put down the Margherita pizza for Alessandra and the penne bolognaise for Romeo. "Buon Appetito." Aromatic basil, tomatoes, and spices made her stomach grumble.

She was curious about his inspiration for the blueprint as he dug into his spicy pasta and chewed. Sauce dribbled down his t-shirt. "Aah, you've got..." She pointed to his top. "Sauce."

He dabbed around his t-shirt. "I should never have sauce again."

Alessandra's gaze lingered on his robust chest, trailing up to his full mouth and considered the way it would feel against her own. She ignored the image and focused instead on her own food. Taking a bite, she savoured the cheesy texture of the sauce, basil, and pepper flavours. "I am curious, Romeo." He frowned. "Why do you keep working overseas away from your family and friends?"

"Okay. Let's make a deal. I share something personal with you if you do the same. One thing for now."

Alessandra shook her head, not ready to disclose anything about her past. "I don't think so. Maybe another time."

He put down his fork and fixed his gaze on her. "Fair enough for now, but to answer your question, I like the escape and recognition of having worked on large-scale projects, and that's it. Nothing more to say."

She got the sense he was hiding something. "Okay, but that didn't sound very personal to me. It seems as if you do this for the excitement and change of routine, but you're gone for months at a time. Wouldn't your family struggle with that?"

He nodded. "Of course they do, but I am thirty years old and my own person. I don't answer to anyone, so I am free to do this now when I'm still young. I cannot see myself doing this twenty years from now."

"I suppose when you're older, you might want the more relaxed lifestyle. You might even be retired by then."

"Possibly, but what about you? Would you want to work overseas in twenty years or would you prefer to be home?"

"I'd prefer to work in Australia, but to have the time for travel after my retirement. I'd love to come back here in the future and see my extended family. I might come here with my brother and father.

Nostalgia, you know." She turned to him. "You could bring your mother and sisters here."

Romeo turned to her. "My family changed over the years, and sometimes it was easier to be distant." He swallowed. "After we left my father, which was hard in itself for my mother, she got even worse with her mental health. She lacked confidence, struggled to leave the bed most days, cried every day, and abandoned her friends and neighbours. My father had put her down for countless years and made her stop believing in herself. My two sisters were a godsend and supported her in every way."

Alessandra's chest tightened. "I am sorry, Romeo. That must have been hard for you and your sisters. How's your mother now?"

He shrugged. "She has her good and bad days, but she's come a long way. Without the support of her friends and family, who knows where she would be."

She pressed her lips together. "When was the last time you saw your father?"

"I'm thirty now, so it would have been about twelve years, or when I was eighteen. He did a lot of damage for at least twenty years, from when they first got married. I still hate the guy and if I ever saw him in the street, I don't know what I'd do to him. He destroyed many lives and I never have the need to see him again."

"It is a shame when one parent's not there for you." She looked down into her lap, not wanting to think about family.

He said nothing further. They ate the remainder of their meals in silence. She wondered if his father was the reason Romeo was distant with her.

Alessandra drained her remaining wine. It soothed her parched throat. "I am so full from that pizza. Are you ready for a few other shops before we head back to the hotel?"

He took out his wallet. "Let's go."

She got up and approached the counter to pay, but Romeo put up his hand. "This lunch is on me. Please."

Alessandra was touched by his generosity. "Thank you, Romeo."

As they walked out, he put his hand on the small of her back protectively, guiding her out of the path of a pushy man entering the restaurant. A tingle ran down her spine.

The last few places they entered were a gallery art store, and shops for pillows and other accessories. Romeo took photographs with his camera for knickknacks and throw pillows Alessandra liked, and she carried a bag full of fabric samples.

As they were walking back to their hotel, he realised he was happy with the pleasant outing they'd had. The day felt comfortable and exciting, and he enjoyed helping Alessandra with her work.

They stopped in front of her hotel room and Alessandra took out her key.

"How about a tea before we head out for dinner later on?" he blurted before he thought about it.

She nodded and opened the door wider, and he headed inside. He sat on the edge of the bed as she put out two cups and glanced at the varieties of teas on the counter. "What kind of tea would you like?"

"A green tea is fine. Thanks." She pulled out the green tea sachets and added them into the cups, waiting for the water to boil. After pouring the water, she handed him the cup and picked up her own. Alessandra sat on the desk chair, across the room.

"I'm curious, Alessandra. You mentioned needing more flexibility in work and planning to start your own business. Are you unhappy with your current role?"

Alessandra blew on the steaming tea and put down her cup on the desk. Her hands fidgeted. "I love my job, but as I said before, I hope to select the clients I'd like to work with. Perhaps even do some work in public housing or women's shelters, as they need good maintenance. If I can set my prices based on what particular groups can afford, I'd be happy to do it. The only issue is finding new clients. Hopefully, this villa will put my name out there and give me credibility."

He angled his head. "I would say you have credibility now."

She shook her head. "Not the kind I need. I have to prove myself with big-scale projects which can support me in the longer term. Then in between the huge jobs, I'll focus on smaller ones."

He gripped the cup. "Sounds like an interesting plan. You get to share your creativity with a wide range of groups."

She nodded. "Creativity and design give me an escape from...things. When I was young, I would be talking to my friends in my room about the latest fashion trends when I got these pictures in my head. Styles, colours, shades, fabric. I told my friends what kind of fashion would suit them, but I had to show them drawings. I started sketching designs, but after a while, I needed to do something that lasted. Clothes don't stay on your body for long. I started changing my bedroom space. I told my dad I needed different window furnishings, softer carpeting, and an entire rearrangement of my room. I had this need to make it my own and my bedroom became my sacred space. I love to create that kind of space for others."

He felt her passion. "It seems as if you needed that sacred space." She averted her eyes. "Your training has paid off, Alessandra. You are gifted and talented, and you have chosen the right vocation."

She sighed. "You didn't believe that in the beginning, Romeo."

He remained silent until he finished his remaining tea. "I can see what you're doing for the villa, the way you choose samples, and your design model. You have more than proven yourself, Alessandra."

"Thanks, Romeo. I appreciate that."

She blushed and realised they could finally be on the same wavelength with this villa.

Chapter 18

MEMORIES

Alessandra and Romeo made their way to the Ponte Vecchio bridge over the Arno River in Florence the next morning. She stopped in her tracks and scrolled through her phone. "It says here that the medieval stone bridge, built in Roman times, is the most ancient and photographed bridge in Florence. It features three arches and two wide arcades on each side, housing famous and unusual shops." They continued to walk alongside the ancient city buildings and approached the bridge. She stopped again and peered at her phone. "It also says that two neighbouring bridges are the Ponte Santa Trinita and the Ponte alle Grazie."

Romeo dodged the multitude of people to keep up with her. "This place features jewellery stores, art dealers, and souvenir sellers. You might find something useful. But I warn you. There are mainly jewellery shops here."

She nodded. Their shoulders brushed and a tingle swept up and down her spine. Those tight, ripped jeans and skin-tight t-shirt pressed hard against his abs and biceps. Slight stubble made her want to dance her fingers over his face and along his inviting, rosy lips. Shaking her head to clear it of Romeo related nonsense, she navigated the crowds until they finally reached the shops. They stopped for a view of the river, taking in the hot summer breeze and gazing out at the clear, blue skies. A group of people stood on surfboards while others sat in kayaks, rowing along the water. Several empty boats lay anchored underneath the bridge. She wouldn't mind joining in, as the water had to be cooler than up here.

They passed clothing stands, pizzerias, gelaterias, and wine shops. People slowly rode their bikes or snapped photographs of the river and landscape from their phones. Alessandra rummaged in her bag for her phone, then took photos of the grassy knolls on the banks of the river. She turned and snapped more photos of the Arno river. Romeo did the same. "The view of the river is so beautiful."

Fixing his gaze on her, he inched nearer. "It sure is."

Alessandra was curious about whether his words had a double meaning, but no, he was only talking about the views. No man had ever called her beautiful.

Heading alongside the bridge, they passed by more shops and browsed outside before stepping into a souvenir store. "I might be able to find a few decorative items for the living room and the other rooms in here."

Romeo nodded. "Lead the way."

After browsing and not finding anything she could use for the villa, they walked inside a jewellery shop where she'd bought a necklace for Mimi, a watch for her father, and a ring for her brother. Romeo stood behind her and browsed the range of diamond rings. Did he have a special someone back in Melbourne? By the way he focused on them while she paid for her items, it seemed as if he had someone on his mind.

Exiting the store, they made their way back into the throng of people. Alessandra's feet were aching in her black flats. Music sounded further ahead, and she spotted two couples dancing to a slow ballad. As they stopped to view the band, Romeo assessed her strangely, most likely wondering why anyone would be dancing in the streets. An elderly man sat on a chair playing the viola, another elderly man played the cello, and a younger one played the acoustic guitar, the music slow and romantic. A viola case lay open by the kerb with coins and Euro notes inside. A young boy with shoulder-length curly brown hair danced between one of the couples. The woman from one of the couples looked familiar. When she met Alessandra's eye, she had a look of recognition, but who was she?

Romeo looked at her strangely. "Are you okay?"

She nodded. "That woman over there looks familiar, but I can't place her. I hate it when I know a face but can't remember the name or who it is."

Romeo touched her briefly on the shoulder. "She's coming this way."

The woman left her partner alone as she wandered in their direction. About in her fifties, she had a short, rounded figure with a bob style haircut and smiling eyes. "Alessandra, is that you?"

Her head jerked back, suddenly realising who she was as she neared. Her mother's old friend. "Maria?"

The woman wrapped Alessandra in her arms, and despite stiffening and remembering her mother, she hugged her back. It wasn't Maria's fault her mother had left. "Oh, Alessandra. It is me." They pulled away. "How have you been?"

Alessandra briefly turned to Romeo who watched her curiously and took a step back. He was respecting her space, possibly knowing it was an awkward encounter for her. "I'm...okay." Her brain failed to form words.

Maria nodded in Romeo's direction then faced Alessandra again. "I am sorry for what happened. I did try to call you after you left Pisa but your father wouldn't take my calls."

She knit her brows. "I never knew about that. I am sorry."

Maria shrugged. "It wasn't your fault. You were just a child, but it is so great to see you after all these years. You're as beautiful as ever."

Alessandra's face flushed, realising that she couldn't ignore Romeo standing awkwardly beside her. "Maria, this is Romeo. Romeo, this an old friend of my mother's." She swallowed, pushing down her uneasiness. "We are working together on a project in Siena and we had to buy a few samples here in Florence."

She put out her hand and Romeo accepted it. "A pleasure, Romeo."

Romeo politely replied. "It is good to meet you, Maria."

Alessandra refocused. "What brings you to Florence?"

She turned to a man who was chatting with a few people in the street dance. "Oh, my husband and I have decided to travel around the northern part of Italy, spending a few days in each city. We have a few weeks then we'll return to Pisa."

Alessandra nodded. "How are your children?"

"Great. Antonio is an engineer and plans to get married in a year. Mateo is a carpenter and has a girlfriend, but who knows if it will get serious."

"That's great. Tell them I said hello."

Maria gave her a reassuring smile. "Listen, about your mother. I haven't seen her since...I am sorry for what happened to you, and I wish that things had turned out differently."

Alessandra fought back tears. "It's okay." She crossed her arms and peered into the ground.

"Can we keep in touch?"

Alessandra's heart constricted, aware of Romeo stepping closer towards her. "Of course." She rummaged in her bag, retrieving a pen and sticky note. "Write your number here."

"Sure." Maria came closer and hugged her again, extending the moment. When she pulled away, she said, "I had better go back. We'll talk some more next time."

Alessandra swallowed. "See you, Maria." As she walked away, she rubbed the heel of her palm against her chest, with an image of her mother's note on the table and the droop of her father's head as he read it. The last time she'd seen her was when her mother left for work and said goodbye, but now that she thought about it, there had been a finality to her tone.

Romeo peered at Alessandra as she drifted in her own world, standing with her arms crossed as Maria walked away. He wasn't sure what to do. Should he say something or get them to walk away? He had never been in a situation where something traumatic had happened to a woman.

The decision was made for him. Alessandra avoided looking at him and said, "Let's go."

She sprinted ahead of him and he hurried to keep up. His eyebrows pulled down in concentration, wanting to console her or offer a kind word. But what could he say when he didn't know the situation? "Alessandra, wait."

Passing by an eatery, she slowed down and ambled alongside him. "Why don't we order some lunch?" She tucked in her upper lip and hugged her arms over her chest. Before waiting for a response, she stepped inside and made her way through the crowd waiting by the counter or sitting at tables on either side of them.

His hand lifted to reach her shoulder but he stopped short. She might not appreciate him touching her when she was clearly upset. "Are you okay?"

Alessandra lifted her head to the menu board. "All good. I might get a chicken roll for lunch." She waited her turn and placed her order then Romeo ordered the chicken roll too.

Once they received their takeaway food, Romeo noticed her furrowed brows and her seemingly frantic need to get out of there. He didn't know what to say as they ate in silence until they reached his car and headed back to their hotel. The short drive was quiet, and Romeo got the sense that she wasn't ready to talk, but he felt that he should say something.

They reached the door of her hotel room and Romeo wanted to be there for her. But maybe she needed to process what had happened, so he shouldn't rush her. Would she agree to dinner with him later? He didn't want to leave her alone tonight.

"How about a late, light dinner in a few hours?"

Alessandra nodded. "Sure. I guess I could eat then. I'll meet you in the lobby at seven." She closed the door in his face. He walked away with a stooped posture and unlocked his own room. Her abrupt departure left an emptiness. He hoped that the few hours to seven passed quickly.

Chapter 19

A STOLEN KISS

Later that night, Romeo sat with Alessandra in the hotel bistro, forking ravioli in a bolognaise sauce while Alessandra dug into a creamy risotto, washing it down with a Lambrusco wine. He sipped on his Shiraz, taking in the dry, crisp flavour, and set it down on his table, admiring the view in front of him.

She wore a low-cut studded black cotton dress, sleeveless and backless, which left little to the imagination. Her eyes gleamed in the soft lighting. She wasn't as talkative as she normally was, and her quiet vulnerability made his chest ache in sympathy.

"Are you sure you're okay, Alessandra? You seem a bit quieter than usual."

She nodded. "I'm fine." Chewing risotto, she peered past him.

The silence was unnerving as he ate his ravioli, barely tasting the Napoli sauce. "I have a tendency to be a good listener when the occasion calls for it. My sisters can attest to that."

Alessandra shifted in her seat. "And why would you need to be a good listener? I said I'm fine." She frowned, then eyed her plate without touching her remaining risotto.

Romeo dabbed his mouth with the napkin and regarded the patrons exiting the bistro, some of them with children and some coupled up. He should ease into her discomfort. "Did you enjoy Ponte Vecchio today?"

Alessandra chewed more of her meal. "Amazing views. What about you?"

"The architectural design is amazing. Did you know that the bridge withstood the war? It is so solid, and has survived the tests of time."

"Great. A lot of things in Italy are sturdy and handmade or hand-carved, particularly the churches like the Duomo."

"Exactly. One dome was built on top of another and is considered to be the largest dome in the world." He paused. "I won't bore you with the design. We can talk about something else."

Alessandra's lips pursed. She forced a grin that didn't reach her eyes. "Why don't you say what's really on your mind, Romeo? I don't like reading between the lines and assuming things."

He drank down his wine then rubbed the back of his neck. Could he be honest with her, given they had to continue working on this project? "I am curious about your friend, Maria, who you met earlier today. She seemed to upset you."

Alessandra winced then clasped her hands together, as if measuring her words. "She was a friend of my mother's and I hadn't seen her for many years."

He rubbed his leg. "I don't know the story about your mother, but I understand when one parent lets you down. It's hard to shake off."

She rested her thumb and index finger under her jaw. "It is hard." She raised her hand to summon the waiter. He arrived instantly. "Can I have another wine, please?"

The skinny waiter nodded. "Certainly, madam." He turned to Romeo. "And you, sir?"

Romeo shook his head. "No, thank you." After the waiter left, he faced her again. "Alessandra? What happened? You never speak about your mother."

She shrugged. "I know." The waiter arrived with her wine and she drank most of it down fast. Her face turned red and her eyes glistened. "I haven't seen my mother since I was ten. I'm almost certain she's still living in Pisa." With a grave expression, she folded her hands in her lap. "My extended family would be able to tell me if I ask them hard enough. Not that I plan to ever visit her."

Biting her bottom lip, she said, "My mother left us a note saying she could no longer cope with being a mother. What did that even mean? You can't suddenly not be a mother."

Romeo's heart clenched. "I am sorry, Alessandra. No child of that age should go through that. Did you get good support from your father?"

She nodded. "He was my rock. My brother too, but it still hurts, knowing she didn't care enough to stay. I wish I could understand it, but I don't."

He knit his brows. "Aren't you curious about her? Don't you need the closure, Alessandra? You could attempt to find her in Pisa if you decide to."

She remained silent as she raised her hand to the waiter. "Another Lambrusco, please." The waiter turned to Romeo.

"I'll have a glass of port, thank you." He left with a nod and Romeo sensed that Alessandra's mood had sunk even lower. Part of him wished he could help her close that chapter on her life and explore what reason her mother had to leave. Not that it was any of his business. Best to shift topic. "The villa's coming along nicely. Very soon we'll be able to arrange those deliveries and have the interior started room by room."

She perked up a little. "I appreciate coming here. I've got so many designs and samples to show Flavio, and the few deliveries we've tentatively arranged."

Romeo's heart warmed at the way her eyes shone when talking about her interior design work. "You are truly talented, and I hate how it took me almost a month to realise that."

Alessandra wobbled as Romeo helped her inside her room. She plonked herself on the couch and pressed her palms on her temples. "We shouldn't have had more wine, or at least I shouldn't. I'm a little tipsy now."

"How about I make us a coffee to clear our heads, then I'll leave you to it?"

She nodded. "Sure. Thanks. I could use a coffee." Alessandra yawned, tucked her legs underneath her, and leaned back.

Rolling her head against the back of the seat she looked at Romeo. He appeared good enough to eat in his tight black pants and crisp white shirt. Why couldn't they share one night together? But they were both involved on this project and anything more would jeopardise that. No, she had to stay focused, and right now, all she needed was coffee and sleep. After what she'd shared with Romeo, she couldn't use him as a distraction from her pain.

Romeo handed her the steaming cup of coffee then drank his own. Alessandra took her legs off the couch, her dress lifting to reveal her upper thigh. Romeo's examination of her thigh made her breath hitch. He peered into his coffee, and she found she missed the warmth of his eyes on her. They drank in silence for a few minutes. "I've had a great time here. I assume we're still going back to work the day after next?"

"I need to get a few bits and pieces. Giuseppe called and would like me to order more flooring because they've come up short. I know where the place is, so I'm happy for us to go our separate ways tomorrow morning."

She nodded. "Okay. We might achieve more. I still need to find other window furnishings and accessories, so I'm happy to go out on my own. So long as I can go to these places on foot."

Romeo nodded. "Great. Tomorrow being our last day here is sorted." He sipped his coffee, gripping it with both hands, then rested the cup on the table.

Alessandra's shaky hands spilt coffee over her dress. "Oh, damn. That burns." Romeo shot up and mopped the front of her dress with the complimentary hotel tea towel. "Are you okay now?"

She nodded, lost for words as her gaze fixed on him with a deep yearning in her chest.

His body moved closer, reducing the gap between them. His hand knocked into hers, sloshing the liquid in the cup. "Sorry. Did I hurt you?"

"No, it's fine."

Instead of moving back he inched forward and reached for her, slipping the cup from her grasp and putting it out of harm's way. Gently, Romeo inspected her hand, caressing her fingers in a slow rhythm, checking for burns. Alessandra's nipples tightened with longing and her gaze drifted between his eyes and lips. His fingers grazed her temple, down her cheek, and traced her upper lip. Alessandra shut her eyes, savouring his touch. An involuntary moan softly escaped, her self-control disappearing, as warmth in her belly made her damp with arousal. When she slid open her legs, he stepped between them and pressed his lips on hers. Tongues glided in and out as the kissing became deeper, hungrier. His hand circled her jaw and worked his way down to her throat and around the curve of her breast. She shuddered with pleasure.

But then her mind rescued her. Sleeping with him could hurt her.

Quickly, she drew away and stood, putting distance between them. "You should go." She looked away, curious about his thoughts.

"I am sorry. If I crossed the line, I apologise. It won't happen again." He moved away, headed to the door, and shut it behind him.

Alessandra dug her nails into her skin and questioned if she'd done the right thing.

Chapter 20

INTIMACY

Romeo headed out of the building supply store after arranging delivery of the extra flooring. He strolled onto the main shopping street of Florence and scanned for any sign of Alessandra, but she wasn't waiting outside the homewares store. He ruminated about last night and how the kiss remained burned into his thoughts. Her soft skin, the taste of wine on her lips, the way her touch made him forget all his troubles. He had never met anyone as beautiful, both inside and out, and he had yearned for so much more than a kiss last night. But she wasn't a one-night stand kind of girl, and he respected that. All he could offer her was casual rather than anything more.

Alessandra appeared in front of one of the shops, gripping her handbag tightly over her shoulder. She wore silky red shorts and a white blouse that showed her feminine curves and slender build. He pushed back the image of her stripped of those clothes.

The scorching heat made him sweat behind his neck and he rubbed his brow, nervous meeting her again after last night. He didn't need any awkwardness between them.

"Hey, Alessandra. Did you find what you need?"

She nodded. "I did, and I believe, for now, we can go back to Montepulciano. Are you ready to do that?"

He hid his disappointment but knew that they had to return after organising as much as they could at this stage of construction. "We can do more later."

As they walked back to the hotel together, their shoulders brushed and he stole glances, occasionally catching her doing the same. The hint of flowers and soap floated on the breeze, and he wished he could inhale her scent by moving closer.

Romeo's phone buzzed in his back pocket. He retrieved it and found Giuseppe's name displayed on the screen. He stopped in his tracks. "Hi, Giuseppe. What's up?"

"Flavio organised for a reporter to check in with you on the project. I understand you were going to leave today, but would you mind remaining there until tomorrow? She's a friend of Flavio's and would like an exclusive about you and Alessandra working together. This could be huge for your careers and for mine. Not to mention some great press for Flavio. The interview has been scheduled for eight o'clock tonight, and she's staying in the same hotel as you two. Sorry, it's last minute, but you realise how impulsive Flavio can be. Margarite, the reporter, is not coming in until seven o'clock and would like to settle into the place first." Romeo ended the call.

The interview meant he could spend more time with Alessandra before they headed back tomorrow. This article would boost their careers and give them more exposure around the world. Today was turning out to be a perfect day.

Romeo turned to Alessandra. "Sorry, but we'll have to stay another day for work purposes." He explained the phone call, and her facial expression suggested she was none too pleased.

"No worries. I guess if duty calls, duty calls. We can do some sight-seeing for a bit if you like."

He nodded. "Great plan."

Romeo entered the hotel at five o'clock after sightseeing and having a late lunch. They had visited the Duomo, the Uffizi Palace and Gallery, and drove past other cathedrals. They both agreed they weren't hungry for dinner but would snack on a few items in the bar fridge. He pulled out a packet of crackers and offered Alessandra one. The way her tongue licked her upper lip got him aroused as they shared the crackers and stood outside on the balcony, the scorching breeze feathering his cheeks. "How about music? You could show me some of your dance moves."

Alessandra chuckled. "I cannot imagine you dancing, but sure I'm game. Try to keep up or I'll be doing it on my own."

He beamed, savouring the light in her eyes. "I was the world-class champion in my Karate group when I was in high school, and that involved graceful movement."

She looked wide-eyed at him. "Karate? I find it hard to believe that you actually had a life away from academics. Where did all that light-heartedness go?"

He relished the banter between them. "Come on. Show me your moves and I'll follow your lead." He walked back inside and Alessandra followed him. Putting on music from his phone's playlist, he set it on the coffee table.

Alessandra swayed her hips and flourished her arms.

"Follow my lead, Mr Bianchi, and as I said, try to keep up."

As he copied her moves, their hips bumped, and he was unsteady on his feet. She caught him as he almost knocked into the table. "I'd better move this table so we have more room," he said.

Alessandra lifted her hands and made a few steps with her feet, which he struggled to keep up with. When a slow ballad came on, they changed pace. "We can't dance to this song, Romeo. Put it on the next one."

He shook his head. "Show me your ballroom moves. No harm in us dancing together." He yearned to hold her and enjoy the music with her.

"Fine, but one slow dance only." She wrapped her right hand with his left and placed her other hand on his shoulder, the heat of her touch travelling down his insides into his loins. The brush of her breath against his skin as she closed the gap between them made him aware of his own heartbeat, with their bodies pressed closely together.

He put his arms around the small of her back as she transferred both hands around his neck, their eyes locking, lingering, fixing on each other and blocking out the world. Her accelerated breath and the way she licked her lips constantly aroused him. Following her lead, his body relaxed in her arms. He needed to be inside her, loving her, connecting with her on so many levels.

When the music changed to a more upbeat song, they ignored it as he captured her face in his hands. He waited for her to resist. When she didn't, he slowly and gently kissed her lips. He moaned in arousal as he pressed her body tighter against him then moved her to the sofa. She rested back as he unbuttoned her blouse and trailed his hands down her neck, kissing her gently around her shoulders and the middle of her throat. Slipping off her blouse, he shifted his head and planted kisses between her breasts while Alessandra stroked the back of his head and breathed heavily. He needed to be inside her, but he wouldn't rush this. He yearned to give her pleasure as his fingers found her inner thighs and teased her. She arched into him and moaned in his mouth as he kissed her hungrily, deeply, their tongues tangled in a web of frenzy and heat.

He slipped off his shirt and unclasped her bra, his hands kneading into her breasts as she shut her eyes as if savouring his touch. Sucking on each nipple, she bucked into him. "What you do to me, Alessandra. And so ready for me."

Slipping off his jeans, he pulled out a condom while she removed her shorts and revealed a G-string that got his nerve endings tingling like crazy. Words failed him as he slipped off her panties and inserted a finger inside her.

"Romeo. You're killing me."

He brushed his lips sensually and slowly between her breasts as his fingers probed inside her gently until picking up the pace, aroused further by her guttural sounds. "I need you to come for me. It excites me when you're excited." He rubbed his thumb on her clit, fixating on the way her tongue brushed over her lips as she caressed his manhood through the last barrier of fabric between them, feeling himself harden and pressing himself tighter against her. She arched her back and closed her eyes, taking rapid breaths, writhing, moaning loudly until she climaxed. When she came, his desire exploded the last of his control and he took off his underwear, put on the condom, and kissed her in the centre of her abdomen before moving inside her. The slow rhythm grew as they melded into each other's bodies. Focusing on the movements, they rocked in a heated dance until they climaxed and fell hard into each other's arms.

He stroked the small of her back and kissed her again. Romeo had never felt this way before with anyone. He couldn't put his finger on exactly what was different about their lovemaking, and he wasn't sure he wanted to. It was just sex, after all, nothing more.

Chapter 21

AWKWARD MORNING

Yawning, Alessandra climbed out of bed. Last night, she and Romeo had attended their interview with the reporter, then made love again in her bed and fell asleep. Turning to the side, she winced at the empty spot beside her. Ashamed of what they had done last night, Alessandra pulled the sheets tightly around her nakedness. Why had he left her? Most likely, now that he got what he needed, he'd be running for the hills. Her heart broke in two, and she bowed her head into her hands and forced herself to not cry. Was he playing games to emotionally compromise and control her? She had imagined that Romeo might be different because of the gentle way he caressed her, stroking her in all the right places, and how he made sure she climaxed as if needing to fulfil all her needs last night.

The way his lips trailed her whole body and how his fingers worked their magic got her aroused again. But where was he now? Was he that ashamed of her that he couldn't bear to see her in the light of day?

A knock at the door forced her to stop dwelling. Quickly, she picked up a robe from her suitcase, wrapped it around her, and opened the door. She sighed with relief. Romeo held a box of food that smelled of cinnamon and chocolate. "What do you have there?"

He forced a smile, scanning her from head to toe. "Cannoli. I thought we could have a treat before we head back."

Alessandra nodded. "Good idea."

He pushed past her without even a kiss good morning, and proceeded to grasp the box of tissues and put the sugary sweets on the table. "Dig in."

Alessandra picked one with the vanilla custard. It was topped with icing sugar and cinnamon, and her teeth sank into the crunchy shell, savouring the sweet and soft texture of the filling. Romeo picked one filled with vanilla and chocolate and shoved half of the cannoli into his mouth as if he was ravenous. He averted his eyes and appeared to rush through his cannoli as they sat in silence during their early breakfast.

"Okay. I'll leave these with you and go shower in my room. I will pack and be back here in an hour." Without waiting for a response, he darted out of there and closed the door behind him.

She was curious about what had just happened. Why had he been so cold and distant, as if the two times they'd made love didn't matter? Did he regret what he'd done? Did he not really care about her and only needed her in bed because of pure carnal desire? She refused to be made to feel like a piece of garbage or dirt. He had not kissed her and had not even acknowledged what had happened between them.

Her mind turned back to the interview with the reporter, which had gone well. The woman had asked them the standard questions about their backgrounds, the status of the build, the sights in Tuscany, and about their future plans. The entire time Romeo had been aloof and distant with her, acting as if they were simply colleagues rather than lovers. But she could understand that he didn't need the reporter to realise what they had done. They had to be professional. But what was his excuse this morning? She deserved better, and now she knew that she'd find it awkward to work with him again.

Romeo showered, his mind replaying last night. It felt right to be melding his body with hers. The way she tantalised him with her tongue and the way she went a little wild as he trailed his lips over her whole body. He had got a taste of her and he wanted more. The only problem was that in the cold light of day, he didn't have a clue as to what to say to her. He didn't want her to have the wrong idea, that they could have a relationship. They had simply got carried away in the moment.

Men and women could have a casual fling whilst away on a break from work, couldn't they? There was nothing wrong with savouring each other's bodies, but why did he feel like crap? Why did he hate the way Alessandra had withdrawn into a shell this morning, barely meeting his eye? Did she regret what they'd done?

He couldn't erase her from his mind. The attraction between them was magnetic, but that's all it was—casual lovers and nothing more. He didn't wish to talk about it when he might hurt her. She had flipped out on him twice when he'd tried to draw closer to her, but now that she had accepted him, did she need more? No, he couldn't consider a relationship now when he knew it wouldn't work out between them. He had a vision and needed to remain focused on nothing but work. If he didn't immerse his head in the game, Flavio might not help him with the drop-in-centre.

Still, his heart felt empty when she left a room or turned away from him. Why could he not keep her out of his mind? They would move through this and discuss other things on their way back to Montepulciano. They had a lot to discuss about work, and they could return to being colleagues and nothing more now that he got her out of his system.

Stepping out of the shower, he towelled off and got dressed. Squinting at the mirror, he spotted a love bite on the side of his neck. Damn! How could he remove that? Hopefully, no-one would spot it.

An hour later, he picked up his travel bag, his stomach churning at the thought of meeting with her again. Could he act casually with her as if nothing had happened between them?

Chapter 22

BANTER

Alessandra walked onto the building site and greeted Giuseppe and Mike. Romeo walked beside her. They had spoken little on the way from Florence, keeping to the topics of work and wine regions in Tuscany. She was stupid to believe he cared about her when he simply saw her as a piece of meat. Well, she would show him that she didn't need him and could act just as aloof. She needed to take back her control. Her vision was work and that would help her through.

They headed inside the caravan and took their seats. Alessandra sat close to Mike and Giuseppe while Romeo sat across from her. Mike rolled out the blueprint.

Romeo pointed to the living space. "Thanks for making that alteration with the door and wall, Mike."

Mike gave Romeo a puzzled look. He scrutinised Alessandra then Romeo. "Happy to do it, man." He tilted his head. "Is everything okay with you two? Did you have a fun time in Florence?"

Romeo nodded then turned to Alessandra. "Your sofa will fit now."

She hid her disappointment, a tightness penetrating her chest. Did he truly have a fun time in Florence or was it a time he'd rather not remember? "Good. Thank you for making that change. I understand it had to be reflected in the blueprint, but it will make our client very happy." She squared her shoulders, her head bowing over the document, brushing off the tension between her and Romeo. "These bits here for the windows, I'll be adding curtain panels to soften the room. I understand Flavio is flexible with the window furnishings, and I need to show you pictures on my phone. These were the thoughts I had for the dining area." She flicked through her phone and showed Giuseppe indoor dining tables. "I'm not sure which ones would accommodate the measurements in that room." Mike and Romeo gazed at the furniture, both nodding. "I'd like to focus on the living and dining areas and work from there." She beamed at Giuseppe. "I am still amazed by Flavio's tastes. He is trendy and up with the latest styles. He has been so easy to work with."

Giuseppe chuckled. "He is a stylish man, my child. Also, a busy man, and if I didn't know his schedule so well, I would never get much of his approval at each stage. Then again, I am aware of his tastes, but if I'm unsure, I will send him a message, Alessandra."

She sat back in her chair, listening to Romeo and Mike talk about the kitchen cabinets, measurement changes for flooring in the other rooms, and plumbing fixtures.

Mike stood and saluted everyone. "I'll keep working and talk to you all later."

Romeo took out a few paint samples for the walls in the dining and living areas. "Alessandra and I chose these paint colours for the walls, but we weren't sure about the exact shading. What do you think?"

Giuseppe pointed to a light peach sample. "This would be more to Flavio's preference." He nodded. "Amazing work. Now, let's talk about the other furnishings in both rooms. I take it you browsed coffee tables, cushions, decorative items, things like that?"

Alessandra nodded. "I have a few different cushions in the car for you to choose from. And these are pictures of rugs, coffee tables, art displays, and decorative pieces we could use." She handed him her phone and Giuseppe scrolled through.

Alessandra rummaged through her bag and took out her notepad and pen. She scribbled down Giuseppe's selections of furniture and other items for the dining and living areas. "Fantastic. I will order those and make sure they arrive here when you're likely to have done the walls and flooring."

Giuseppe rubbed his hands and rose from the table. "I better go supervise the hard workers." He turned to Romeo. "Come and meet me in about ten minutes. I need to show you something about the cabinets in the kitchen."

"Sure, I'll be there." Romeo fixated on Alessandra after Giuseppe left. "Listen, I have to say that I appreciate how well we can work together now. It was a different story in the beginning."

She nodded, aware of the way he moved forward, closing her in. "I appreciate that too." Taking the plunge about Florence, she asked, "Did you not have a good time in Florence?"

His eyes darkened. "What do you mean?"

She massaged the base of her neck. "When Mike asked you about it, you only nodded and shut him down. I was just curious, that's all." Looking past him, she waited.

He shrugged. "It was fine. Florence is a beautiful place with a lot of great sights, and we got the job done. Now, it's back to the reality of work." He rose. "I need to talk to Giuseppe. I will talk to you later."

She watched as he fled the caravan with a heaviness in her body. He had not once mentioned how he'd had a great time with her and kept it neutral. Why did it feel like he had punched her in the gut?

Romeo and Alessandra got back to the apartment after a long day's work at the site on Friday. He had gone through the specifications with the team, and Alessandra continued working on her design model, walking through the building site and discussing how she envisioned the interior design in the two rooms they'd discussed with the contractors. He managed to avoid conjuring images of her curvaceous body or the sweet way she tasted when he kissed her. But ever since they got back, things had been awkward between them, and he didn't know how to be with her anymore. Florence had been fun, and he struggled to admit that to her, but he didn't need her to have new notions about them.

Alessandra opened the fridge, looking through the contents. She took out a few eggs, cheese, asparagus, mushrooms, and capsicum. "How about a vegetable frittata for dinner? There's also ciabatta in the pantry."

"Sure. I adore frittata and bread. Can I help?"

Alessandra hesitated. "Okay. You can slice the mushrooms and I'll cut the cheese."

He nodded. "Okay." Moving over to the sink, he washed his hands after she'd washed hers then retrieved a knife from the drawer, accidentally bumping into Alessandra as she picked up another knife. He ignored the warmth of her body and the way the curve of her breast fit in the loose-fitting top. "Sorry."

She blushed. "All good."

He put a chopping board on the counter, washed the mushrooms in a bowl, then proceeded to cut them."

Alessandra peered over his shoulder while she cut the cheese into small blocks. "Hey, that is not how you cut mushrooms. Here, I'll show you." Brushing against him, she pressed her lips together and squinted, appearing sexy as Hell, as she concentrated on the slicing. She stopped. "You have a finer slice this way." Shaking her head, she said, "Who taught you how to cook?"

He chuckled. "I make a mean pasta with the best meatball sauce you can taste."

"I doubt that. I'm sure you buy the sauce from a packet rather than make it yourself."

"Hmm. You think? My sisters will attest to the fact that I have my own select dishes I can cook. But then again, a woman's job is in the kitchen, right?"

Alessandra put her hands on her hips. "Excuse me?"

He threw his head back and laughed. "I am joking. After all, I have never met a woman who is as multi-talented as yourself." Alessandra stiffened, and her face reddened again. She got quiet. Did he say something wrong? He had to fix this as he didn't like the sudden tension in the air. Slicing like she taught him, he asked, "Is this better now?"

She relaxed again. "Of course. Great job."

Once they finished cutting and Alessandra cooked the frittata, they sat down to eat, with the warmed bread resting on a chopping board.

"This is delicious, Alessandra."

"Thanks. It was something my mum taught me before she...well, she did something right."

At least she was talking about her mother now. "You won't starve."

"Hmm, but you will." She took a bite of the soft and cheesy texture, her lips wrapped around the fork and chewed slowly. He couldn't help being jealous of the fork and yearned to taste her again. They finished their meal and talked about Florence.

He couldn't keep having this tension between them, so Romeo broke the ice a little. "I did have a fun time with you in Florence, Alessandra." He inched forward and stroked her cheek lightly. "Did you like Florence too?"

She nodded. "Very much. It's an exciting place, and I especially appreciated the bridge and the shops, even if most of them were jewellery stores. I managed to achieve a lot for the villa. And then there was the..."

He inched forward, and broke her words as he smashed his lips against hers, not able to control himself any longer. His tongue tantalised her and he bit her bottom lip gently. His hand touched the bottom of her jaw as he delved deeper into her mouth, their lips licking, exploring, and devouring.

Alessandra pulled away. "We're not in Florence anymore, Romeo. I think we should stop right now."

He couldn't blame her after how awkward it had been between them. This would be more complicated if they continued this. "You're right, Alessandra."

Chapter 23

KEEPING IT CASUAL

A lessandra tossed and turned in her bed. When she stared at the clock, the display showed three o'clock in the morning. Flustered, she pulled the blankets off her, sweating and exhausted from the heat. Heading to the kitchen, she poured herself a glass of water and drank it down, spilling some of it down her cleavage. "Damn." She shouldn't have been walking around in her flimsy, transparent pyjamas. Picking up a tissue from the box on the counter, she wiped in between her breasts. Romeo's door opened and his footsteps approached. Appearing in the corridor, his eyes lingered on her chest with his lips parted. She swallowed and put aside the tissue.

"Did I wake you?" said Alessandra.

He rubbed his eyes, and as she stepped back, he neared the sink, grabbed another glass from the overhead cupboard, and filled the glass with water. She couldn't help but notice his black board shorts fitting snugly around him and his stubble prominent in the moonlight.

Putting the glass in the sink, he said, "I'd better get back to bed." But instead of leaving, he stood transfixed and lifted his hand to her cheek. "It is very hot in here, isn't it?"

She nodded, arousal forming a lump in her throat. His wet lips and strong gaze enticed her to take a step forward. Maybe it wouldn't hurt to enjoy each other one more night. She didn't have to make a big deal of it and was strong enough to keep it light and fun. It didn't need to be serious when, surely, they could both relieve stress. It wasn't like he'd promised her anything after their previous encounters. No, this could be something two mature adults could enjoy.

Alessandra reached for the hand caressing her face, then slowly she brought his hand to her lips and moaned. He inserted an index finger into her mouth, and she licked and sucked it to her heart's content until he pulled it out and replaced the finger with his lips, kissing her hungrily and devouring her lips. He moaned, then guided her out of the kitchen and into the bedroom without words. The heat rose as he rested on top of her and lifted her blouse, intent on tasting all of her.

Alessandra sensed a body beside her and slowly opened her eyes. She stiffened when spotting Romeo. Her mind turned back to last night and how they had made love. Romeo had devoured her entire body. She'd never felt so loved and worshipped, as if he had never shared intimacy like that with anyone before. Now that she had her wits about her, she wondered if it had been wise to sleep with him again. Was she completely out of her mind to give in to temptation and be sucked back into his masculine web?

Romeo stirred and she lay absolutely still so as not to wake him. She had to leave here and shower, and she didn't need to be gawking at his naked body with its rippling muscles, hairy chest, and...scars? The daylight illuminated scars on his stomach and upper arm.

Lifting the blanket, she was about to hop out of bed when an arm gripped her hand. "Hey, gorgeous! Where are you going?" Romeo was half-asleep. Alessandra rested back down on the bed and turned to him.

"Go back to sleep. I'm having a shower."

He grinned cheekily. "Let me join you." He pulled the blankets off, crawled across the double bed, scooped her into his arms, and carried her to the shower. "Before you try to leave, I'm holding you." The comfort and strength of his arms enticed her and she needed more.

Once they reached the bathroom, he turned on the water and they walked inside. Romeo picked up the soap and washed her body, the suds sliding down the curve of her breasts and nipples. He lathered her back as he leaned into her, then trailed the soap down to her legs and in between her thighs, teasing her with two fingers until he put the soap aside. Rather than let Romeo take full control, Alessandra retrieved the soap and rested a hand against his chest. She drew the soap over his chest then down to his navel until reaching his manhood, lathering the soap up and down as Romeo leaned back, his breath hitching. He closed his eyes and his manhood hardened, but before proceeding further, he opened his eyes, and pulled her to him. His teeth nipped at her bottom lip and he kissed her hungrily, caressing her buttocks and moaning against her mouth. She dropped the soap and wrapped her fingers around his manhood as he hardened while he devoured her mouth until her lips became swollen. His fingers prodded and teased her mound. She slid her fingers down his arm and over his, pushing his hand tighter against her. As much as she had wanted to resist him before, their strong connection threw her logic out the window.

"You drive me crazy, Alessandra."

He moved down to his knees, looking up at her with something akin to affection.

Even though she would attempt to keep this thing between them light-hearted, she questioned if he truly cared about her? But she needed this.

Feathering her skin, his fingers ran down from her abdomen, around her hips and waist, to trace the privacy of her inner thighs. Inching into her, he shifted his head and wrapped his lips around her mound, probing gently with his tongue while spreading her legs wide. The warmth from his mouth was soothing as his tongue tantalised her. She pushed his head deeper inside her. The guttural noises he made had her clutching his hair, then tenderly tracing his jawline as she emitted small gasps. She moved in rhythm to his tongue, flicking in and out and tantalising her until climaxing. He shifted his body up, kissing her hard on the mouth, tasting herself on his lips. He then caressed her thigh, lifting it to give him better access and guiding his penis gently inside her. Eyes locked on each other, they got into a gentle rhythm until crying out simultaneously in orgasmic bliss.

After their shower, Alessandra dressed while watching Romeo put on his shirt. She peered at his scars again. "Those scars, Romeo."

He winced and turned his head away. "Courtesy of my father, but I would rather not get into it." He pressed his lips together. "I might head into town and buy a few groceries. Do you need anything?"

She hated how he had changed the subject. "No, I'm fine." She lifted her chest. "My friend, Mimi, is thinking of coming down for a couple of weeks. Can she room here?"

Romeo nodded. "Won't it be a bit crowded, if you know what I mean?"

Alessandra wasn't sure how to take his question when he didn't seem to need anything more than a fling. Even now, he had become cold and detached again. "Are you saying you'd like to do more of this?"

He pressed his lips together. "This is a way to unwind and let go of work at the end of the day. That's it. I mean, this is just fun for you too, isn't it? No strings, right?"

Alessandra had a sudden onset of nausea but pushed it down. Why did his words cut her like a knife? She didn't need to end up with a controlling man like him, anyway, but he spoke as if he didn't care about her. But then again, she had gone along with it, and they hadn't promised each other anything. They were two consenting adults, and if she didn't become too attached, he couldn't hurt her, right? "No strings. If that's the case, then having Mimi here won't cramp our style. It's not like we need to do this again. We've had our fun, and now we can move on with work and focus on that. I don't need distractions anyway, and I really have to do more work today. Later, I might take a walk."

Romeo's eyes darkened as he lifted his t-shirt over his body. "I can take you anywhere you need to go rather than walk. If you wanted to go somewhere specifically."

She waved her hand. "No need. It's just a nature walk." Stepping into her underwear, she noticed Romeo's eyes land on her inner thighs, and she reddened. Why was she self-conscious now when they'd been intimate before? Part of her felt dirty and humiliated as this was the first time she'd had casual sex with a man. She hated being anyone's dirty secret.

Romeo gazed again. "Are you all right with our arrangement?"

She laughed. "Of course. My goodness, Romeo. I like to have fun just as you do. I am not in the headspace for anything right now, and us having sex was great, but it's over now. We've had our pleasure, and Mimi can stay here without cramping anything."

He squinted. "Our pleasure doesn't need to stop. We can still do things to each other without anyone else being aware of it. After your friend leaves, we can enjoy each other's bodies again. Lord knows I've loved yours."

Alessandra could barely breathe as she walked over to the dressing table, brushed her hair and began walking to the exit. Why did his words hurt and make her feel devalued? "I'll go for that walk now rather than later."

Romeo said, "Wait. I can come with you."

She frowned. "I need time to myself. Give me some space." She hurried out and didn't turn back, not wishing to continue this conversation. She should never have slept with the man. She sure knew how to pick them.

Carrying her phone with her, Alessandra made her way outside, walking around the trees and mountainous terrain, basking in the warm wind, and savouring the warm glow of the sun. She took giant steps into the unknown, making sure to take a different track than where Romeo would be driving to. She couldn't bear to see him when he had brushed off the sex as if she didn't mean anything. But why was she overthinking this? She could be just as casual as him and would not get attached.

Her phone buzzed in her pocket and she retrieved it, answering a video call from Mimi. "Hey, Alessi. How are you? Where are you?"

"Hi, Mimi."

"What's wrong? You look pale. What happened, girl?"

She didn't really need to get into it, but Mimi always had a way of restoring her confidence. Maybe she needed some tender loving care from her friend. "I sometimes hate Romeo so much."

"I will need a few more details to follow, Alessi. What happened?"

She explained today's and last night's intimacy and Mimi's eyes widened. "I feel like he only sees me as a body and nothing else. I don't think he ever cared for me. He's just like the others, Mimi."

"How much do you like Romeo? From where I'm standing, it seems like you're in love with the guy."

She shook her head firmly. "Of course I'm not in love with the guy. I care about him, sure, but a part of me feels like he only sees me as someone who gives him physical pleasure and nothing more. I told him you were coming, and he said it would be too crowded for you here. What a pompous, arrogant jerk!"

Mimi's eyes darkened. "I'm sorry, Alessi. I don't have to come if you don't want me to. I probably would be in the way."

"No, you wouldn't. You'd be a good distraction, and we can go out."

"Listen, about Romeo. If he didn't like you, he wouldn't have slept with you so give him some credit. I am sure he cares about you. He may just have a focus right now, and that's the villa. Let him get to know you better. You've still got a few months left on your contract, so who knows where it can go."

Alessandra sat on the hilly ground, holding the phone up. "I have already told him that we're done with sex and that I just need to focus on work. I can't let him upset me anymore, Mimi. I have to protect my heart."

"I understand, but don't make the mistake of thinking he's like the others. He might not be, and besides, when I come over, I will decide if he deserves your criticism."

They spoke about their respective families, and when she ended the call, she lifted her face up to the sun and soaked it in. She would no longer let a man dictate who she was. It was time she defined her own worth. If only Romeo's mere presence didn't set off her libido.

Chapter 24

SUPPRESSION

Over a week later, Alessandra waited in front of the apartment for her friend to exit the dark-grey sedan—Mimi's rental car for the next two weeks. Her friend wore long, black boots and tight-fitted black shorts, with a skin-tight white singlet top. Mimi threaded long, slim fingers through her glossy, sandy-blonde hair that flowed down to her lower back. Alessandra believed Mimi belonged on a runway as a model instead of working as a fashion designer.

Alessandra rushed to Mimi and wrapped her arms around her. "I missed you, Mimi, and you look amazing, as always."

"As do you, my love. As do you." Alessandra wore drab, casual attire compared to her friend: casual cotton shorts and a worn t-shirt over thongs. But today, being Friday, was her day off to give the building team time to work on kitchen cabinets and structural fixtures around the living room. She had a few days free to spend with her best friend. Mimi peered past her. "So where is the infamous Romeo?"

Alessandra's chest tightened. "Shh. He might hear you. He's just in the kitchen, cutting up some fruit to welcome you. He's excited to meet you."

Mimi put a finger around her jaw. "Oh, and why is that?"

"Because I talk a lot about you, and he is curious. Now let's grab your suitcase from the boot. Do you have much?"

Behind her, Romeo yelled out. "Let me do that." He approached Mimi and shook her hand. "Hello. I am Romeo, and you must be the famous Mimi I have heard so much about?"

Mimi's eyes widened. "Yours truly, Romeo. The pleasure is all mine. And thanks for picking up my stuff. It's a rare find to have a man help you these days."

Alessandra shook her head. "It might be because you pick the losers at those nightclubs you frequent. It's time to focus on different locations, don't you think?"

Mimi shoved her gently on the shoulder, sighing. "And why would I do that? Who needs to commit to one man when you can have your choice? It's a little like choosing a bland white fish over salmon. It is just not done, girl."

Romeo laughed as he picked up the hefty suitcase from the boot. "You were not wrong about your friend, Alessandra. She possesses the personality of someone who is always running on well-charged batteries. An admirable quality."

"Why, thank you, dear Romeo." She strode inside the apartment, her eyes darting around the interior. "Wow. This is an amazing place. Are you sure there's room for one more here?"

Romeo set the suitcase inside Alessandra's bedroom. "All perfectly fine, Mimi."

Alessandra squeezed her friend on the shoulder. "We'll share the double bed."

Mimi nodded. "I appreciate the gesture." She picked up a slice of kiwi fruit from a silver platter and devoured it.

Alessandra pulled out a beer and handed it to her friend. "Here you go. You must be thirsty after your long flight."

"Thanks." She unscrewed the cap and drank a lot of the beer down.

Romeo rubbed his hands together. "Listen, I have to head to the construction site but might see you later tonight. It was a pleasure meeting you, Mimi."

"And you too, Romeo. Have a great day."

He left them alone and the room seemed empty without him. Over the past week, she had decided that having casual sex was not a big deal, so they had had sex two more times. But it was becoming harder and harder each day to believe that she would no longer be with him after this project ended.

They sat down at the table and picked at the fruit while Alessandra drank down a glass of water. "I decided to go into the city once you've had some sleep. You must be exhausted after the long flight."

She nodded. "I am a little, but first I need the goss. Tell me about you and Romeo. Have there been any developments?"

Alessandra chuckled. "We've been keeping it casual. Keeping it light means no-one gets hurt and having fun." Did she sound convincing?

"Hmm. I noticed how much he stares at you. I wonder if he'll be able to say goodbye to you after this work ends." She devoured a whole strawberry then picked up a cube of rockmelon. "This is so refreshing."

"Like you said last time, he might like me but it's more as a friend than anything else. It is what it is—friends with benefits. I don't mind. It suits us for now. That way, we can both be clear-headed as we work, and no attachments."

"Are you sure about that? I mean, I get you, Alessandra. You let emotions guide you, girl. Will you be able to let him go in the end? Or am I going to have to pick up the pieces?"

She shook her head, eating a strawberry. "It's fine. I won't let myself become caught up in anything. I assumed, in the beginning, that he was too serious for my liking, but he's become relaxed these past six weeks. We still have a few months to go. Plenty of time to squeeze leisure after work but not so much time that we'll be hung up on one another. All fine."

Mimi squinted at her and gave her a reassuring grin as if not believing a word she had said. This time, Alessandra would make more of an effort to protect her heart.

Romeo had his hands on his hips, surveying the door separating the living room from the dining room. "We need the glass sliding doors to go here, Mike. Did you order the glass doors?"

Mike nodded. "Sure did. Alessandra requested the doors to have some rustic-looking vertical blind over it, one that blocks out the sun. We organised delivery of the window furnishings and the doors."

"Good. This villa is starting to take shape, and before long, I'll be back on my other projects and that will be that."

Mike put the drill aside and walked over to him. "What will be what?"

Romeo's mind turned to Alessandra and how much he would miss her once they stopped working together. It was best this way. "Nothing, Mike. Let me check the other side and see whether the flooring is right in the dining room."

Mike held up his hand. "Wait up." He tilted his head. "You're falling for her, aren't you? To the point that you don't want this project to end? Tell me the truth, man."

"Ridiculous," he lied. Mike was right. He didn't wish for this project to end, but only because he appreciated staying in Tuscany and not for any other reason. "Oh, by the way. Her friend Mimi arrived and she is a knock-out. She appears to be your type, Mike."

Mike sighed. "Oh, stop changing the subject. You're lucky I have work to do and don't have time to argue with you, man. Now let me show you what else we've got planned for today." They entered the master bathroom, but Romeo's mind was on Alessandra and the way she could please him in so many ways. She was even in his dreams. Hardly a minute went by when he wasn't conjuring her in his mind. Soon she'd be a distant memory, and he knew it was for the best.

Chapter 25

A STERN WORD

Over the weekend, Alessandra and Mimi drove around in her hire car and visited a winery in Montepulciano, the markets, cafes, and restaurants. She missed the sex with Romeo. Now Monday morning, there hadn't been time to sneak away.

Flashing back, Romeo was cupping her neck with his hands carving through her hair. She imagined how his lips and hands explored her curves, and how he whispered his desires with, "I can't get enough of you."

Romeo trailed his hands over her, scrutinising every inch of her body with presence and deep-seated need. Even now, her heart warmed as she imagined him touching her in all the right places on a permanent basis to be totally loved and cherished. She had never been valued by a man, but when she and Romeo made love and savoured each other's bodies between the sheets, she could have sworn he felt something more. Or was it only her imagination and wishful desires? But no, it had to be only the sex he got pleasure from, nothing deeper than that. He was lost in the moment of his desire. Why did she have to read things into a simple situation?

Alessandra got ready for work and added lip gloss in front of the bathroom mirror. The door opened and clicked shut behind her, and as she turned, Romeo came up to her. He wrapped his arms around her and leaned in for a slow, tantalising kiss.

"I have missed your beauty this weekend. If we didn't need to go to the site, I would take you to bed right now," Romeo said as he brushed a hair strand out of her face.

Alessandra chuckled. "I miss our time too, but Mimi's here for two weeks and I can't be gallivanting with you while she's here. You will have to steal these moments with me."

"Hmm. I guess I can wait, given that we do have a few more months of pleasure." His eyes travelled from her head down to her feet as if he was undressing her. "Luckily, I have a great imagination." He winked. "Are you ready to go?"

She tingled. "Can you give me ten minutes? I have to rearrange something on my design model."

He nodded. "Sure thing. I'll be in the living room." He turned and opened the door, and she scrutinised his taut buttock muscles as he left. The confident swagger made him all the sexier. Shaking her desire away, she made her way to her bedroom and opened her laptop. As she waited for it to boot up, she remembered they'd be receiving a delivery of a few materials today. It would give her a better vision of how the villa was taking shape. Her heart burst with excitement as the villa became the real thing, and it was her sweat and creativity which could make it a success in the public eye. This could go a long way to hooking clientele for her own business. It was the only thing she had going for her right now.

Romeo spotted Mimi sipping coffee in the kitchen while flicking through an interior design magazine. "What's your plan for today?" he asked.

She offered an easy grin. "Not sure yet. Possibly go to some of the other villages. I read Pienza or Suvereto can be interesting with its wine tasting and spas."

He frowned. "Suvereto is about two hours away. Are you sure you want to drive that distance?"

She nodded. "I don't mind driving, and I am here on holiday, so why not? Tomorrow I might go to Florence or Siena, or wherever this scorching wind takes me."

He opened the fridge and picked up a plum. Biting into it, he savoured the soft and juicy texture, then picked up a napkin from the counter. He sat across from Mimi. "You are welcome to come to the site and meet the workers."

Mimi nodded. "Maybe tomorrow or the next day. I'll let you know, but I do appreciate the offer, Romeo." She took another sip and looked back at Romeo, asking, "Alessandra mentioned how you two are kind of together."

Romeo winced, not expecting the change of topic when they'd been talking about sights around Italy. "Nothing serious, but we enjoy our time together."

Mimi stared into her hands. "Listen, I am not sure what you know about Alessandra's past, but she has been scarred by her ex-boyfriends. Controlling men, and I am looking out for her. Her ex-boyfriend nearly destroyed her and made her feel like garbage, putting her down verbally all the time and making her second-guess herself. Sometimes, I believe emotional abuse can be more damaging than physical abuse because it lingers when your physical pain can heal." Mimi huffed.

"She deserves to be loved and respected. Alessandra has an amazing beauty and value both inside and out."

Romeo's skin turned cold and he swallowed. He hoped Alessandra was still happy with their arrangement. Had she said something to Mimi? "Alessandra and I are taking it easy and not moving into anything deep. We both don't need a relationship, and she agrees with this casual arrangement."

"Hmm. I understand that, but Alessandra has a tendency to fall hard for men, especially when they lavish attention on her. "I don't want her to get hurt."

He chuckled nervously, not understanding how he could make it clearer to her. "No-one will get hurt because it's casual, nothing more. She understands the arrangement."

She sighed. "Is it?"

"Definitely casual, and she won't read anything more into it. Once this project is over, we will part ways and move on with our lives. Nothing more, nothing less." She remained silent as she kept flicking through her magazine, her shoulders drooping. Mimi appeared to want to say more, he was sure, but she remained tight-lipped.

Alessandra finally emerged with her bag and briefcase in hand. "Have a nice day today, Mimi, whatever you decide to do. Tell us when you'd like to visit the site."

Mimi beamed. "Sure, girl. You have an amazing day." With a brief nod to Romeo, she said, "And you too, Romeo."

Romeo walked alongside Alessandra as they reached the car and he drove off.

"Are you okay?"

She shifted her body. "Is everything all right between you and Mimi? I sensed some tension in the air."

"All fine." He didn't want to discuss it as it might put strange notions in her head. All he needed to focus on was their work and nothing else. It might have been ideal to have Mimi here for two weeks so she didn't get further attached to him. The space would help.

Chapter 26

ANGER

Alessandra sensed Romeo had distanced himself from her. In the bathroom, he had been easy-going and pleasant, but now he had transformed into his original stoic robot form. What had happened in that ten minutes between him and Mimi? Did she say something to him? She hadn't heard their conversation from the bedroom, but she was sure Mimi might have said something to upset him. She wouldn't bring it up now when they had to focus on work.

Once they reached the building site, she exited the car and greeted all the men. A huge truck parked in front of them, and two bulky men were hauling a glass window out of it and laying it on the ground. It was wrapped in foam sheeting. The driver held out a clipboard and approached Giuseppe who inspected the remainder of the windows. Another man dragged another window and rested it next to the other one. Giuseppe checked the measurements of the window and shook his head.

Romeo approached. "What's wrong, Giuseppe?"

"This is the wrong size and not the one Alessandra recommended." He turned to her. Her heart stopped. She had ordered with the measurements he gave her and cross-checked the size herself. She was sure she measured it right based on the blueprint.

Romeo peered down at the windows, then at the blueprint Giuseppe was holding, and shook his head. He glared at Alessandra. "Did you order this measurement? They're too big and won't fit in the living space."

Alessandra swallowed as her mind reeled, questioning what she had ordered. Immediately, she got angry. What was he blaming her for? Romeo had ordered her to ring the company to have them delivered when that part should have been his job, or at least a collaborative one. "I can't remember, but I was sure I wrote down the right measurements. Maybe they made a mistake." She asked the delivery man, "Can you bring us the right ones?"

He turned to his colleague. "Listen, we're just the delivery men. Take it up with the company."

Romeo glared at Alessandra then at the man. "You cannot leave this here. Take it back and we will arrange for the right ones to be delivered."

"No can do. We have other deliveries to make and we're on a deadline. I don't have time to bring these windows back. Sorry, *amico*." He made his way back inside the truck and drove off.

Mike looked at the man driving away. Giuseppe was on his phone and walked away to talk to someone while Romeo put his hands on his hips, staring at Alessandra.

"How could you be so stupid and order the wrong windows? This is going to delay construction. Who knows when we'll get the right windows?"

Alessandra's body stiffened and her feet remained frozen on the spot. "I am so sorry, so sorry. I was sure I ordered the right ones. The company must have got it wrong." Hands shaking, she briefly shut her eyes, trying to regain composure.

"Oh, whatever." He stormed off and approached the contractors on the other side of the villa. She turned to Mike.

"Don't worry about it, Alessandra. Let him cool down. This might set us back but it won't make much of a difference." He squeezed her shoulder. "Giuseppe's handling it. Besides, it should have been either Giuseppe's or Romeo's job to order those windows. Anyone can make a mistake like that."

Her erratic breathing caused her to be light-headed. "Thanks, Mike. I just need a minute."

She headed to the caravan and shut the door, then sat on the bed and bowed her head. How could she make a mistake like that? Unwelcome thoughts raced in her head. Her ex-boyfriend, Johnny, had ripped her to shreds when she added chilli to his sauce after cooking for him one night. He had called her stupid for not remembering how he hated chilli and got sick from it. The rage in Romeo's eyes reminded her of Johnny, and history repeated itself sometimes. The moment Romeo called her stupid was the moment she decided she could no longer do this casual thing between them. She didn't need to become further attached to him, having realised he was not the right man for her. Why risk falling for a man who liked control to a fault? After today, there was no chance she could be with a man who belittled her.

Later that evening, Romeo waited until Alessandra finished speaking to Giuseppe, who wrapped his arms around her as if he was consoling her. He gazed from his car as his mind wandered back to his rage earlier. Why had he become angry with her? Where did that even come from? He hadn't meant to call her stupid, but in that moment, he had pondered what Mimi had said. She made him angry and had no right to tell him how he should feel. If he kept Alessandra at arm's length, then she'd keep away from him. Was that what he was doing? Trying to hurt her before she could hurt him? That was ridiculous, but he knew she'd be better off without him. Was this truly his method of pushing her away? Was he making up an excuse?

Sure, they would be delayed in construction, but it wasn't a huge loss. He had made the situation bigger than it was, and he knew without a doubt that Alessandra was smart and funny, and kind and loving, and...*Stop it!* This was not the time to focus on all her endearing qualities. He had to keep his distance from her. He didn't have any control around Alessandra, and he needed his control back. She was too independent and fiery for his own good, and he didn't need that. He didn't want that.

Romeo didn't do emotions, but he was worried that she was changing him and making him into something he didn't need to be. He had to have his wits about him and focus on his priorities.

Alessandra walked towards him. "I'm sleeping in the caravan tonight. I think we need space. Geraldo said he's been with his girlfriend this past week and won't be using the caravan."

He flinched. "What? Why?"

She shrugged. "As I said, we need space." She avoided his eyes and shuffled her feet on the ground. What was so interesting down there?

He steeled himself. "I am sorry about before. I didn't mean to lash out at you. You don't need to sleep in the caravan. You don't even have your clothes."

"I'll only be here for one night. I'll talk to you tomorrow." She turned away from him and strolled to the caravan, his heart sinking in his chest. What did he do? Did he upset her so much that she needed to stay in the caravan?

Shaking his head, Giuseppe approached Romeo. "How could you be so harsh to Alessandra? I just spoke to the company. Apparently, they accidentally swapped our order with someone else's. Alessandra didn't make the mistake, Romeo. The company did. You need to apologise." Giuseppe stormed away.

Romeo clenched his hands and bowed over the steering wheel, hating himself with a vengeance. Driving to the nearest bar, Romeo knew he couldn't go home tonight to that apartment without her. To even consider returning there without Alessandra made Romeo's stomach knot. If Mimi was there, he'd likely get an earful. But why did he care? It wasn't like he was going to continue this casual affair between them. It seemed as if Alessandra wanted nothing more to do with him casually, but why did it give him an empty sensation in his stomach rather than a sigh of relief?

Chapter 27

A PERSPECTIVE

L ater that night, Alessandra and Mimi sat inside the caravan. Her friend crossed her legs while pressing her back against the bedhead, and Alessandra had her legs stretched out beside her.

"I cannot believe he got angry with you like that. He should be the one staying here the night instead of you."

Alessandra picked up her mobile phone. It was eight o'clock but no messages. An ache in the back of her neck gave her a headache. "Then I find out it was the company's mistake and not mine. He could have at least got his damn facts straight instead of jumping down my throat."

Mimi shook her head. "But he apologised?"

"He did, but it was a weak one. I don't know how I'm going to work with the guy again, but I have to be professional and act with maturity. I can do that."

Mimi bit her bottom lip. "Can you, though?" Alessandra remained silent. "I have a confession to make, Lessi."

Alessandra turned to her friend, curious. "What is it?"

Mimi put up her hand. "Before you get all angry on me, I only did this because I have your back. After Johnny hurt you..."

"Spill it, Mimi. I can take it." She got the sense that Romeo might have had a few choice words from her friend. Mimi explained and Alessandra's gut tightened.

"Are you serious, Mimi? I had the feeling you might have said something, but that was a little over the top. Now, he probably believes I like him more than he likes me. He is judging me right now."

Mimi took her hand. "Listen, girl. I've got your back and I only did it out of love. Do you remember how distraught you were over Johnny, and how you've been upset with your mum all these years? If you don't let these go, how can you move forward? If Romeo's the man for you, then he won't be judging you. He'd be respecting you and making the right decision by you."

Alessandra knew Mimi was right. She'd only had her best interests at heart. But time and space would hopefully make her realise that Romeo was a passing fancy, nothing more. Then why did she have an ache in her heart, imagining Romeo's beautiful features?

Romeo guzzled down a glass of beer. "Another one," he said to the bartender.

The man behind the counter sported a moustache and wore glasses. "Don't you think you've had enough for one night?"

Romeo inched forward. "I am paying, so respect my wishes."

The bartender poured another glass of beer and slammed it on the counter, some of the beer spilling. "Listen. Instead of wallowing, why don't you talk about whatever's bothering you."

He picked up his glass and downed half of it, wiping his mouth with the back of his hand. His stomach tightened, visualising Alessandra's full lips, the curve of her hips, and the shine of her hair. He loved twirling his hands through it. "Nothing, man. I'm good."

The bartender wiped the counter. "It's a woman, isn't it? Always is with men here."

Romeo could share a tad of his story as he needed someone to tell him he hadn't made a mistake. "I got angry with someone over a misunderstanding and now she hates me." He talked about the specifics and the bartender nodded.

"I hear you, man. But if you look at it from her perspective, she had every right to get upset and leave you stranded on your own. You didn't get your facts straight."

"I apologised. What more could I do?" Romeo drank down the last of his beer, realising he should stop there as he needed to drive.

"Maybe this casual thing doesn't work for her. Women like men to be honest about their feelings. Have you been honest?"

He nodded. "Of course. I only want casual." The man grunted. "I'd better get going before I get drunk. Thanks for the advice."

Before driving, he took a walk to clear his head, then headed to the apartment. He turned on the lights and looked over the silent, empty apartment. Alessandra's design model sat in the living space and her cardigan rested on the edge of the couch. Scents of rosemary and lavender filled the air. The scent of her.

As he walked into her bedroom, he focused on a set of clothes lying on the chair and her jewellery and accessories lining the dressing table. His heart ached and his shoulders deflated at how empty the apartment seemed to be. She was only going to be away for one night, so why did he act as if it was forever? Crazy. It must be because he was

settled into a routine of her being here, which was why it seemed silent
now. It didn't mean anything more.

Chapter 28

JEALOUSY

T he next weekend, Romeo was flipping through an architectural magazine when Alessandra sat beside him. She wore a tight-fitted red blouse and skinny jeans.

"I have barely seen you this past week, Alessandra. You've been busy."

She gave him a forced smile. "I have, but I like I said before, we should just remain friends, Romeo. We've had a good time but let's keep this professional from now on." Her eyes darkened fleetingly. Did she honestly want to stop this casual thing between them? "Anyway, Mimi would like to go over to a wine bar, and she plans to meet some sexy Italian guy. She needs me to be her wing woman."

Mimi strutted inside the living room. "What are you saying about me, girl? I am not easy that way."

"Hmm. You think so, Mimi?" She faced Romeo and got up. "I'll talk to you later. If Mimi meets her man, I will sympathise with the guy."

Romeo chuckled, his stomach clenching at the idea of her possibly meeting another man. "Enjoy yourselves." He watched her as she left, and the curvaceous form of her body aroused him further. Did she truly want to keep it professional between them?

Mimi waved to him. "Bye, Romeo. Don't miss us too much." He laughed and shook his head.

He headed into the kitchen and cooked himself a steak that had defrosted in the fridge. Mike and a few other contractors had asked him to go out, but he wasn't in the mood. His eyes darted around the apartment, noticing her flat shoes by the couch and the lingering smell of her perfume. He had not slept well this past week and kept waking up due to having dreams of the times they'd laughed over his dancing, the way she wrinkled her nose when brainstorming designs, and how they had cooked beautiful meals together, bantering in the kitchen. They hadn't made love in over a week and he missed that. Had she forgiven him completely for the other day?

Romeo had fallen asleep on the couch with the TV blaring in the background. A banging noise awoke him. He peered at his watch in the semi-darkness, noticing the time. It was four o'clock in the morning.

Rising, he spotted Alessandra's red blouse lying on the floor outside her bedroom. Why was her top on the floor? Her door was shut, but as he put his ear next to the door, moaning reverberated and the bed creaked. His mind scattered to a thousand thoughts as he realised that Alessandra was having sex with another man. No, she wouldn't betray him like that, would she? Not that they were dating, but she wasn't the type to have sex with a random stranger. But the evidence was clear—her top was lying on the ground. She must have met someone at the wine bar, but he didn't believe she was the type to have a one-night stand. Was she? How well did he truly know her? Voices in the background broke his heart in pieces as he heard, "Oh, baby, baby! Yes, yes." He couldn't be sure it was Alessandra's voice but it had to be her. She needed another man and he wasn't good enough for her. Was that why she stopped their casual affair? Because she needed to have this kind of freedom in Italy?

Clenching his hands, he stomped to his room and packed a bag. He could no longer stay in this place with her and have her flaunt her sexuality in his face. This couldn't be happening all over again, could it? He had to move out of here, and fast, before his rage got the better of him and he broke something in the apartment.

His chest burned, and his fingernails dug into his skin as he cursed under his breath and shook his head. Did she not care about him at all? He couldn't believe she'd go behind his back and cheat on him. Was it cheating when they weren't a real couple? Who cared? She did the wrong thing, given they had recently been together. He could never be with her ever again. It was over.

Alessandra stretched out her arms as she tossed and turned on the hard bed inside the caravan. It was four o'clock in the morning and she couldn't sleep, her mind turning to how she wouldn't be in the apartment when Romeo woke up. It didn't go as planned when they had met with Mike and his contractor friends at the wine bar. Mimi had flirted with him until the contractors left and they were on their own.

Mike had been kind enough to let Mimi down when she'd proposed they spend a night together at his apartment, but he mentioned how he wasn't staying alone. He also hadn't wanted to impose on Alessandra's space in the bedroom, but it was a chance for her to do something nice for her friend. Why not enjoy her time and spend a night with Mike? She could use more of her own space too. It was becoming harder to be near Romeo since she decided not to continue their fling. Part of her needed Romeo to miss her, and this way, he might appreciate her much more. Not that she expected more out of him, but a part of her hoped.

She didn't believe Romeo would mind Mike and Mimi spending the night together in the bedroom, given Mimi was leaving in less than a week.

She laughed at the way Mimi fell in love with her blouse and suggested they change tops. Given Alessandra wasn't the type to pick up random strangers, she didn't believe she needed to attract any men tonight. In the car, before Mimi drove off, they swapped tops and Alessandra had worn Mimi's tight black singlet top well. But now, she found herself thinking about Romeo and how much she would have liked to be with him tonight. She had forgiven him for calling her stupid as she realised he had been upset about something and hadn't meant it. She hadn't made the mistake with the window in the first place.

Pulling the blankets up high, she shut her eyes and allowed herself to dream of her and Romeo making love. It was the next best thing.

Chapter 29

MISTAKE

Romeo yawned as he woke. Sunlight peeked through partially drawn blinds, and he suddenly remembered where he was; in a motel in Montepulciano. His body clenched as he recalled what had happened last night. Hearing Alessandra make love with a stranger she'd picked up was gut-wrenching.

His body ached, and his chest tightened at the notion that she considered so little of him that she would sleep with someone else. This didn't have to mean a thing. It wasn't like he was in love with the woman. If she needed to have sex with another man, who was he to stop her? He couldn't offer her anything more than sex anyway.

As he rose out of bed, he checked his mobile phone on the bedside cabinet. It was ten o'clock and he'd had at least a few hours of sleep. His phone suddenly buzzed. The display flashed Mike's name. He answered the call. Why was he ringing him today? Surely, he'd like to catch up on sleep, being it was a Sunday.

"Hey, Mike. What's up?"

"Where the hell are you, man? Don't you sleep at the apartment?"

"I'm in a motel."

"Why would you leave? I saw your bed hadn't been slept in." He didn't need Mike in this mess so said nothing. "Are you there?"

"Yes, and since when is it a crime to need my own space?"

"But Alessandra's not at your apartment so why would you be out?"

Romeo knit his brows, confused. "What are you talking about?"

He huffed out a breath. "She stayed at the caravan last night to give Mimi and I an amazing night together at your place. She is so beautiful. I'm in love, man." Mike explained the series of events last night.

Romeo sighed with relief, realising that it hadn't been Alessandra having sex but rather Mike and Mimi. How could he be so stupid, believing she would go out and pick up a random stranger? She wouldn't do that, would she? "There's been a misunderstanding, Mike." He explained his version of events.

Mike chuckled. "For a smart guy, you can sometimes be stupid. Why would she have sex with someone when she obviously cares about you? Even though you're both just casual. Besides, Alessandra wouldn't do that. She has principles."

"Where is she now?"

"She's back at the apartment. Mimi can drop her off so you two can talk, or would you rather come here?"

"No, we'll need privacy. Mimi can bring her to the motel."

"Okay. Text me your address."

"All right. I guess I need to sort this out. Thanks, Mike." He ended the call then texted Mike the address of the motel.

Alessandra waved goodbye to Mimi then made her way to the third floor of the motel. Her heart beat fast at the notion that Romeo had obviously cared enough about her to be upset and leave. She had laughed when Mike and Mimi explained how he had left in the middle of the night, believing that Alessandra had slept with a random man. How could he think so little of her?

Knocking on the door, she steeled herself for what was to come. When he opened the door, he took her breath away at the way his hair was neatly combed and how the stubble around his mouth made him sexier. His woody cologne drew her in. The softening of his eyes tugged at her heart as his gaze lingered on her with a sorry expression. His dark eyes made him appear lost as he moved aside to let her inside. "Hey, Romeo."

Romeo glowered. "Come in. We need to talk."

She thought that there was an ominous tone to that statement, but she wouldn't jump ahead of herself. She admired the huge window with Holland blinds drawn, the timber double bed, the shaggy carpet, and the old-style armoire. "Nice place."

Romeo sat on the couch with Alessandra beside him. "I am sorry I got the wrong idea. It's just that I saw your red blouse lying on the ground and I thought..."

She shook her head. "Mimi and I changed tops in the car. I take it Mike told you the whole story?"

Romeo clasped his hands together. "He did, and I'm sorry to have believed that...you understand."

Alessandra pursed her lips together, leaning forward. She wanted to yank him by his shirt and slap him after the way he had thought so little of her. "Don't you know me well enough? I don't pick up random strangers at bars. I have never done that and don't plan on starting now. So why would that be on your mind?"

He squared his shoulders. "I am sorry, but I saw your top on the floor. What was I to believe? How would I know you changed tops with your best friend?" He sighed and turned away briefly as if he had every right to believe she'd been easy with men. Why couldn't he think it was Mimi rather than her? There could have been an explanation about the top, but he had instantly thought the worst.

She got up and paced the carpeted floor, approaching the window. She pulled up the blind and a little sun seeped through the window. "It's dark in here." She stood by the window with her hands on her hips. "Why would you come to a motel when you have your own bed? They couldn't have been that loud, could they?"

"I didn't need to cramp anyone's style so I came here." His eyes told her otherwise, and she knew he was lying.

"No, you came here because you were jealous. Weren't you?"

He scoffed. "That's ridiculous, Alessandra. If you want to go galli- vanting with other men, it's your prerogative. I can't stop you."

She nodded, her chest constricting. "Right. So if I went and picked up a random stranger right now and had sex with him, you'd be okay with that?"

He avoided her eyes. "Of course. You are free to do as you like. It's not like we're in a relationship. If I want to sleep with another woman, I would do it too."

The pain of his words stabbed her like a knife, and she was nauseous. How could he be so cold and detached about this? "I don't believe you, Romeo. You came here considering I was with another man and you were jealous. Admit it."

He shook his head, clenching his hands as he got up and moved within inches of her face. Staring into her eyes, he said, "I told you this is a casual thing between us, so don't go making it out as if I should care. I don't have a stance on what you do. Once this project is over, you will go your way and I will go mine." He averted his eyes. "In fact, you were right in saying that we should stop this fling we have and focus on our work. I don't need you to believe this is more than it is."

She pressed her lips together, her legs unsteady. "Why would you even consider I give a damn about you? If it's what you'd like, I am happy with that arrangement. It's not like there aren't plenty of other fish in the sea. As you said, I am free to do as I like." She gave him a mocking grin and made her way to the door. Turning back around, she glared at him. "Even if we were together, the trust obviously isn't there. You didn't trust me last night and believed I would go from one guy to the next. You should have known me better than that. But you don't know me at all, Romeo."

"Where are you going? I need to drive you back."

Facing him with a frown, she shrugged. "I think I'd prefer to find my own way back. It's not that far. Why don't we make a fresh start from now?" She opened the door and heard him cursing under his breath. After reaching a public bathroom downstairs, she sat inside the cubicle, bowed her head and cried. What had she just said to him?

Chapter 30

RUMINATIONS

Clipboard in hand, Alessandra analysed the crème holland blinds in the living and dining room areas. She turned to Mike. "Luckily they didn't take too long delivering the right windows."

Romeo spoke to Giuseppe about the plumbing fixtures, intermittently watching her. She couldn't think. It had been a few days since the discussion in the motel. A distant voice called to her.

"Alessandra, did you hear me? It wasn't your fault with the windows. The company stuffed up and they've apologised. Didn't Giuseppe tell you?" Mike said.

"Yes, he did. I was almost sure I gave them the right measurements. The company made me second-guess myself, but I'm glad it wasn't me."

Mike turned to scowl at Romeo who was watching him with his palms out, as if asking what was wrong. "He can't admit his mistakes sometimes. He is stubborn that way. He had no right to talk to you like that. Even after the other night, he shouldn't have believed what he did when I know you care about him." Focusing behind her, warmth relaxed his features. Turning to investigate, Alessandra greeted Mimi.

"Hey, Mimi. What are your thoughts?" Alessandra asked.

Mimi tilted her head and pondered. "I could do better." She chuckled, then Mike retrieved her hand and kissed it. "Just kidding, girl. I love it so far. Can't really imagine when it'll be done but it is taking shape. Excellent work." She faced Mike with a hungry gleam in her eyes. "You too, Mike."

"Thanks. So when are you leaving for Melbourne?"

"I've got a few more days, so why don't we make the most of it?" asked Mimi as she stroked Mike's shoulder.

Alessandra needed Mike's attention. "Listen, about the cabinets. Did Romeo order the ones I mentioned to you or did he go with the other option?"

He glanced at Romeo in the distance. "The other option. They're in now." She walked with him to the living area. "Listen, I understand you and Romeo have called it quits but don't let it affect your work. You two need to be communicating."

Mimi joined in, shaking her head. "The guy can't seem to take his eyes off you, Alessandra. He is so smitten with you, and yet you two cannot seem to communicate." She peered down. "I am so sorry for the misunderstanding we caused. Because of it, you have stopped seeing each other. Why don't you talk to him again?" She gave Mike a look and he left them to join the other men.

Alessandra exhaled. "What's the point, Mimi? He made it clear he doesn't care about me. I refuse to be put down that way again. From here on, I am only going to be with a man who respects both my mind and body. I won't settle for anything less. Romeo is just a man who loves and leaves. As simple as that. But in my case, he never got past the casual stage, so I have to accept it."

"But you have feelings for him, don't you?"

Alessandra swallowed. "I might, but it doesn't matter. It's not reciprocated and I am okay with that. I've got my friends, my family, my work, and my future business. I don't need anything else." The words sounded hollow and a sense of emptiness filled her. Why couldn't she eradicate Romeo from her mind? She changed the subject. "What about you and Mike? You appear to be going strong?"

Mimi nodded. "We are, but ours is just a fling, nothing serious. We might catch up when he returns to Melbourne. We'll see. But we're both on the same page, which is where you should be with Romeo. Tell him how you feel. I mean, girl, how do you know he's not just scared of a commitment? He might care about you just as much you do him." She stayed silent. "His behaviour shows he cares, even if he can't express it."

"I refuse to be the one to make the first move. If he cares about me, he can approach me. I have enough on my mind anyway."

They made their way around the site and inspected the other rooms.

Romeo couldn't stop staring at Alessandra, wearing that short summer dress with flats, her hair tied up in a short ponytail which complimented the smooth outline of her neck. He remembered kissing that neck and the rest of her, and struggled to remain focused. Why couldn't they continue their casual relationship? Enjoy the pleasures of life. Women had to always make it about emotions, and he needed to keep it simple. If it wasn't easy, people got hurt. But he missed her body aligned with his and the way she kissed the outside of his bicep or traced her fingers down the middle of his abdomen and down lower. *Stop it!* Romeo admonished himself. He had to shake out these images and focus on the cabinets.

Giuseppe hammered a nail into the kitchen cabinet before it was set up inside the room. He waved at Romeo. "Can you hand me my toolbox, Romeo?"

"Here you go. Are you sure that will hold?" Giuseppe nodded. "And does Alessandra like the type we chose? We had those two alternatives, but this one works best. She is okay with that, right?" Romeo remained quiet.

Giuseppe scoffed. "Seriously, Romeo? She is right over there. Go talk to the lady."

He shifted, holding the blueprint as he inspected the door of the living space. "She is busy. Besides, I can't see her anymore."

"Well, go find her. Anyone can see how much you care about her. Tell her how you feel and be done with it already. Buy her roses."

He chuckled. "Right. Roses." He walked over to one of the contractors who was tall and bulky. "Listen, Marco. You need to fix this door. It's not secure enough."

Marco nodded. "Sure, Romeo. I'll have it done once I've fixed this window."

Romeo roamed the remainder of the villa and ended up nearing Alessandra. She was in a deep discussion with another contractor while Mimi stood with her arms crossed. His heart stung at how easily she had managed to forget about him to focus on her work. Wasn't that what they were supposed to be doing, though? She could, so why couldn't he?

Chapter 31

OVERSEAS OFFER

Romeo sat in the apartment and lingered over a text message on his phone a week later. The words reverberated in his brain as he gripped his phone and scrutinised the message, his heart hammering due to a mixture of thrilling adrenaline and fear. It had become real and surprising after a phone call from one of the most established and prominent building companies. Three sentences to change his life: *As per our telephone discussion, we would like to offer you a job in Germany. A six-month project. All expenses paid.*

Without much consideration, he had accepted the offer on the phone, but he started to wonder if he had done the right thing. It was a long time to be away from his family, friends, and...her. His mind was playing tricks on him. He was no longer in a casual affair with Alessandra. Germany was the right thing to do. A way to distract himself from having to possibly bump into her in Melbourne. He'd keep it to himself for now as the project wasn't for another four months. The only person who knew about the phone call was Mike, and he had preferred not to give his opinion about the offer.

Romeo had time to finish up this job and move on to his next one.

"Are you ready for the party?" Alessandra asked.

Shifting in his seat, Romeo put away his phone, not ready to break the news about his new project. That could wait. "Sure." He gazed at the way her red, silky dress augmented her feminine curves, stately and classic like the curvature of a beautiful building, the dip of her sexy cleavage akin to a well-structured slide, her tanned, slim legs, high and thin, which showed a short split on both sides, and her proportional breasts. He imagined peeling the dress off her body and making slow, sweet love to her. Alessandra's curves were as captivating as curved architecture, akin to the Bilbao Guggenheim Museum with its multiple curved structure, evoking more emotion rather than its angular features.

Romeo appreciated and respected her personality, comparing it to a nicely decorated façade and beautiful interior building that created mystery as you uncovered each room, each space slowly unravelling the wonder. Her mind reminded him of a Zen garden that flowed to give a sense of space, evident that she had a beautiful nature, an amazing mind, and easy-going personality.

He got up from the sofa and they exited the building. The backless dress made it difficult not to watch as her hips swayed with each step. He yearned to trail his fingers over her skin and make her scream his name. What was he doing? They had agreed to be friends and not lovers, but she was driving him insane with her attire.

The short drive to Giuseppe's house for his fiftieth birthday was silent as they listened to soothing jazz. Intermittently, Alessandra would turn his way as if she was going to say something but then held back.

Every night, he struggled to sleep as she was always on his mind. He missed her. Not only in a physical sense but in an intellectual sense too. She had distanced herself and he craved their banter and camaraderie.

Arriving at the house, they walked alongside each other as Romeo held the small of her back. Her wedged heels made her a little wobbly on the grass until they reached the paved concrete path heading to the house. Before they had a chance to ring the bell, Enza answered the door. "Hello, Alessandra. Romeo. You look nice. Come in." She swung open the door and Romeo followed her in. Alessandra trailed in behind them. A rendition of an old Italian ballad reminded him of the way his mother had danced to this song with him as a young boy in her better days.

A gigantic 'Happy Fiftieth Birthday' banner on the red living room wall made the space vibrant. The room had a table covered with snacks including Italian sausage, cheese, crackers, prosciutto, and an assortment of antipasto on two platters. Alcohol, water, juice, and soft drinks were also on a nearby table and inside several iced coolers. Photos of Giuseppe as a younger man and boy hung on string down the length of the ceiling.

Moving into the living area, Romeo waved to Mike and a few other contractors. He slapped hands with them. Mike was missing Mia after she'd left a few days ago, doing a barely passable job of hiding it, but the two were planning to catch up after the villa was built.

Romeo picked up a cold beer then stood next to Mike while Geraldo, the contractor who was older and stocky, interacted with Alessandra.

"Hey my man. Have you thought more about that offer to work in Germany after this?" Mike asked.

Romeo stiffened. He wasn't ready for Alessandra to hear about it when there was no point. They would be going their separate ways. But then again, what was the real reason he didn't need her to know? Did he consider she might change his mind about the offer? Or was it the opposite? "I am thinking of going, Mike."

Alessandra's face flushed. She put down her wine glass on the nearby table. Focusing on Geraldo, she said, "Poor Enza looks busy. I might see if she needs help." She avoided his eyes and gave Geraldo a reassuring smile.

Romeo sensed that her leaving might have been an excuse to get away from him. The stricken expression broke his heart in two. Did she care if he left? It wasn't as if they would keep in touch. He should have told her himself out of respect for their friendship. He had to talk to her about this as he didn't want to leave on bad terms. Geraldo caught him up in a conversation about the villa, so it was twenty minutes before Romeo could go find her.

"Excuse me, guys." He hastened into the kitchen, watching Enza pull out a tray of lasagne from the oven. "Let me help you with that."

Enza moved aside, beaming as he grabbed a nearby towel and took the lasagne, placing it on the countertop. "Thank you, Romeo." She gave him a quizzical look. "If you're looking for Alessandra, dear, she's outside."

He nodded. "Thanks, Enza."

Finding her in the back garden, Alessandra was hunched over a table gazing at her hands. She had beautiful hands. He yearned for her to glance up at him.

"Alessandra. Are you okay?"

She forced a grin and glanced at him. "Of course. Just needed some air. The wine I drank must have gone to my head."

He knew she was lying. He saw it in the way the light had dimmed from her eyes. "I didn't want you to hear about it that way. I'd only told Mike and would have told you eventually."

"It really is none of my business what you do after this project. It's your life, not mine. But I thought you had the drop-in centre to build?"

He nodded and sat beside her, savouring her subtle perfume and the fresh soap scent in her hair. "I can do that virtually at the start or possibly delay it. Flavio will understand."

She crossed her arms, her hands shaking. "Don't you like to control everything? Are you just going to hand over control to someone else while you're overseas?"

He knew he'd be giving up control of his project by working virtually, but his ambition to work overseas again overrode the need for control he'd be giving up. "I am willing to overlook it or it can wait a few months."

"Fair enough. If it's what makes you happy, good luck." She pressed her lips together, peering out at the night sky with a hint of daylight remaining.

"Thanks." He dared to ask the next question. "Did Enza need help or was there another reason you left when you did?"

She rubbed her arms as if she was cold. "I was surprised, and as I said, it's your life and I have no claim over you."

He yearned to hold her in his arms and reassure her that her life would be better without him. "I should have told you, and I'm sorry. Can you forgive me?"

She chuckled. "Nothing to forgive."

"Come here," he said.

She turned to him, and he wrapped her in his arms, stroking the back of her head and savouring the way it felt so right to hold her. *Damn!* He would miss her, but he had to get over it eventually—out of sight, and hopefully out of mind.

When they pulled apart, he needed to close the gap again. His chest tightened seeing the vulnerability in her eyes. Why was she crying? He ached along with her sadness, his body nearing hers as he caressed her forearm. Alessandra briefly closed her eyes as if savouring his touch.

He hated himself for causing her pain and wanted to take it away. When she opened her eyes, he ran his fingers around her jawline, the heat in her eyes evident. His body took over and he crashed his lips onto hers. Before he could truly appreciate the softness and taste of her lips and mouth, she pulled away and glared at him.

"What are you doing?"

"I'm sorry." Why couldn't he tell her the truth; that he had a craving and a need for her that was not rational? He could not stop thinking about her.

She got up from the table. "I don't need your pity, Romeo. I am not some damsel in distress you need to save. Don't read this wrong because I don't care what you do with your life. It's your life." Alessandra stormed back inside.

Romeo balled his hands into fists. He had given in to his desire when there was nothing between them. There could be nothing between them, not ever. So why did all the warmth leave when Alessandra wasn't near him?

Chapter 32

CRAVING

Later that night, Alessandra had her arms around Mike as they danced on the living room floor to an Italian ballad. Romeo was talking to Enza while intermittently watching Alessandra with concern. The contractors and a few of the other guests had left, and only the five of them remained. Giuseppe's children had gone to bed and it was time they left, but she relied on Romeo to drive her back.

She hated herself for showing emotion earlier. It was a strong reaction to Romeo leaving after this project. Part of her held hope that maybe he would want to see her again once this work ended, but he was leaving. Was he leaving for Germany so she wouldn't have the chance to contact him?

She didn't need to admit that she was falling in love with him, but these emotions had a mind of their own. She couldn't sleep or eat, and even when he was around, she was envisioning a life of marriage, a house with a fence, love, and children, but Romeo was incapable of love. He only loved himself.

Mike gazed at her strangely. "You and Romeo have been funny with each other all night. What is up with you two? Is it this project in Germany? Are you going to miss him?"

She shuddered as he held on to the small of her back. "No, of course not. He has his life and I have mine. It wasn't like we had this serious love affair. It was just casual."

"Hmm. Are you sure about that?"

She nodded. "Yes, I am sure, Mike. It's all fine," she lied.

Romeo said, "Can I cut in?"

Mike nodded and pulled away. "All yours, man."

She didn't want to make a scene, so she smiled politely and ignored the way his strong arms pressed against her back and how the scent of his body held a hint of spicy cologne. His hand over hers made her chest flutter, and she could barely breathe as their faces were within inches of each other. The kiss earlier was magnetic, but then she remembered why he was kissing her. To take advantage of her vulnerability so he would have the upper hand. He always needed control, survived on it, but she couldn't have another man who controlled her or made her feel devalued again.

Their bodies melded with the music. She might hate him right now, but she appreciated how he felt against her. After this, there would be no more dancing nor intimacy. She was done with his mixed signals. She deserved better than that.

"I'm sorry," he said. "Can we talk about this later?"

"What more is there to say, Romeo? You're leaving. No big deal."

Romeo sat cross-armed on their apartment's couch later that night watching Alessandra, who handed him a cup of coffee while she clasped her own. He took a sip and wished he knew what was on her mind as she sat beside him.

His mind replayed their dance together, the way she melded nicely into his arms and the way their hands remained glued to each other's. It felt right, but theirs was a no-strings attached affair, and at the end of the day, he could say goodbye without emotions involved. Maybe they could be together one more time for old times' sake.

He put his cup on the table and turned around to face her. Rubbing his hands together, he pressed into his knuckles at a loss for words. But he needed things out in the open as this project would be ending soon. He couldn't leave her on bad terms. "I know we don't have much time left, so I need your opinion about how you really feel with the news."

"As I said earlier, it's your life, Romeo and I have no say in what you do after this. We're both adults."

"I was going to tell you, but I never found the right time. I owed you that at least since we've become friends. I apologise for not telling you sooner."

He wished he could touch her one more time as he missed her. Was it a crime to crave one or two more nights with her? "We like each other's company, and I hope we can remain friends in Melbourne at least."

She rested back on the sofa and faced straight ahead. "I don't think so, Romeo. It's too..."

His curiosity was aroused. "Too what?"

She shook her head. "Nothing. It's nothing."

He had to let her know that he hadn't been using her, but in this moment, she was probably putting him in the same category as her ex-boyfriend who had emotionally abused and devalued her. He respected her as an independent woman. "I like you, Alessandra, and you have to realise it was not purely physical for me. It wasn't."

She scoffed. "Right. You only wanted my body but nothing more than that before. It sounds physical to me."

"What more do you need then? How can I prove that I like your mind and your personality, as well as your body, Alessandra? Tell me."

Alessandra took a slow, deep breath. She remained silent for a minute. "I don't know, but I want a real relationship with a real man. One where I am valued and loved and cherished and respected. I can't go through....I won't go through less than that ever again." He frowned. "My ex-boyfriend, Johnny, was controlling. He didn't believe I could start my own business. He said I wasn't smart enough or savvy enough or beautiful enough. Twice I asserted myself with him, and twice he broke my lip and jaw. When he tried a third time, I slapped him across the face to ward him off, but then he threatened to sue me for assault. I was trying to defend myself."

Romeo's shoulders stiffened and his heart warmed for Alessandra, suddenly needing to protect her from any pain. He wanted to rip Johnny's heart out as she avoided his gaze as if ashamed. What did she need to be ashamed of? It was that creep who needed a strong dose of punishment. "I am sorry, Alessandra. What happened to him?"

"With the help of my friends, Mimi especially, I got the courage to leave him. I reported him to the police, and for a while, things escalated to the point where he wouldn't leave me alone. I stood my ground and he gave up. Last I heard, he moved interstate to Queensland after his reputation got tarnished by me."

He nodded, feeling the sting of her words. "You deserve to be cherished and more. You're a magnificent woman with a range of beautiful qualities, and I am sure that one day you will find that man. And you're right, you need a real man in the long-term, and it's not me."

"Right. Of course I will. One day I will find a man who won't just use my body for his own selfish pleasures. Or find that man who is not ashamed to call me his girlfriend or wife. One day I will find that man. I guess the sooner we finish up here, the sooner I'll find that man."

He felt the anger raging beneath the surface even though he could see that she was fighting to keep it together. He didn't blame her for hating him. Hell, he hated himself. "Don't underestimate yourself, Alessandra. You deserve happiness."

She shifted in her seat. "What about you, Romeo? Do you plan to find that special woman one day, or do you plan to be single for the rest of your life?"

He swallowed. "I have other goals for now. I have enough to keep me distracted and it's all I need." As soon as it left his lips, he knew the words were hollow, but he couldn't be the man she needed.

She got up, finished the last of her coffee, and glanced at him. "I hope you and your ambitions have a nice and happy life together, Romeo. Goodnight." Alessandra stormed off. The conversation had not gone to plan. Neither of them had found any closure, and the little he could offer her was definitely not enough. Maybe space was the best thing for both of them.

Alessandra tossed and turned in bed, unable to sleep. She rose and booted up her laptop then video called Mimi.

"Hey, girl. What's up? I've got a few minutes before my meeting."

Alessandra's shoulders deflated. "It's Romeo. He's leaving for Germany." She recounted their discussion and how Romeo didn't want a relationship.

"Oh, girl. Now, you listen to me. I could see with my own eyes that Romeo likes you more than he wants to admit. You mentioned he'd been burned before, so perhaps give him time to work things out in his head and heart. There is a part of him that cares, and more space might do the trick. If he is your destiny, girl, then you'll be together."

"I doubt that, Mimi. He can't even admit anything. He's still as robotic and emotionless as ever. I don't even know how he truly feels about me."

"I hear you, girl. But don't give up. Enjoy the rest of your time in Italy, and I'll call you soon so we can talk more about this."

"Thanks, Mimi. You go to your meeting. I'll be fine. We'll talk soon."

She ended the call, wondering whether Mimi was right. Would space make him realise that she meant something to him? Who knew?

Chapter 33

DETACHED

Romeo turned to the reporter, Marguerite, and answered her questions. A cameraman stood behind filming them. Alessandra noticed them from the caravan. "The villa is coming up beautifully, and we envision it will be finished in the next two months."

The reporter nodded. "And what are your plans for after this project?"

He hesitated. "I have a commercial project in Germany for at least six months."

She asked a few questions about the specifics of the building until he froze at her next question.

"Is there anyone important in your life?"

Romeo intermittently looked at Alessandra whose eyebrows raised. What could he say? He sure did have an interest, but he didn't need to give anyone the wrong idea. "No, I'm free and single."

Alessandra opened the door to the caravan and shut it behind her. Was she upset by what he had said? Did she truly need more?

"Tell us about the type of flooring you have used in the different rooms? You have created a rustic appearance, haven't you?"

"Exactly." *Stay focused*. "The flooring is a Baltic-type timber. The hardwood's durable and perfect. The wood will stand the test of time." He went on to describe the rooms and space.

The reporter asked further questions. She turned to the cameraman and put up a hand to signal him to stop the video. "Where is your co-worker, Alessandra? I would like to speak to her as well."

"She's inside the caravan. I can go and bring her out if you like."

She waved a hand. "No, she is coming out now." Quickly, Marguerite adjusted her microphone while the cameraman changed the focus on his camera. When Romeo turned around, Marguerite pushed past him with a neutral expression.

She introduced Alessandra to the viewers. "I am curious about what you have done so far, Alessandra?"

Ensuring that he moved out of the shot, Romeo paced the ground in front of the caravan with his hands on his hips, shutting out the conversation. He couldn't stop the part of him that ruminated about what it would be like to hold her right now. If the timing was different or he was a different person, he could imagine a possible life with her.

He focused back on the interview and gazed at Alessandra who gestured with her hands, describing her part in the project. She had created a design that spoke of beauty, impeccable skills, a diligent work ethic, and design experience. He had underestimated her.

"And do you have anyone important in your life, Alessandra?"

She shook her head. "No, no-one important. At least not important enough to mention. Any man I have would need to treat me well, show respect and real love, and they are truly rare in this world. I need a man who can respect me for my mind more than anything. Something long-lasting and real." Romeo frowned in her direction, but Alessandra ignored his existence.

"I can understand that," the reporter said. "We all envision our dream man that way. Now, how about the future of the villa. What more needs to be done?"

Romeo left the site and went for a drive. He was not going to listen to Alessandra put him down, even if indirectly. He hadn't used her for his own selfish needs. He had liked her and still did. Why didn't she believe him when he said he liked her? He had never intended to once show any disrespect towards her, so how could she target him so coldly that way?

Later that day, Alessandra searched for Romeo so they could leave, but he was nowhere to be found. She hadn't seen him all day and she wondered where he had gone. Part of her felt guilty for being so blunt during the interview, but at the time, she was hurt by his comment that she wasn't important to him. She had been triggered as Johnny came to mind. In hindsight, she realised she might have been hard on Romeo. Maybe she shouldn't have started anything with him.

Giuseppe approached. "Alessandra, I can drive you back to the apartment."

She nodded. "Where is Romeo? I haven't seen him all day." She walked to his car near the caravan and entered the passenger's seat. Something didn't feel right, and Alessandra's heart beat fast.

Giuseppe started the motor and drove to the apartment while adjusting his rear-view mirror. He briefly turned to her. "He said he wasn't well and took the day off. Did you have a fight?"

She didn't need to air their physical relationship to Giuseppe but she was sure he knew there was something between them. "Not really, no."

Giuseppe frowned. "I have noticed that you two care about each other."

"He is busy focusing on his career. He'll be leaving for Germany soon enough."

"I know it's none of my business, Alessandra, and let me know if I am stepping out of line here, but Romeo cares about you more than he likes to admit. He is stubborn that way."

She nodded. "If he did care, he wouldn't just leave for Germany like that." He would tell her, treat her with respect, and stop trying to use her just for her body.

"I am sure he has his reasons. Don't give up on him. You two live not far from each other back in Australia. Maybe you can work things out?"

She shook her head. "By the time I return, he'll be leaving for Germany and I won't see him ever again."

He grinned. "Why don't we stop for a coffee nearby before you go back? Give you two space?"

"Sure." She ignored the ache in her heart.

Chapter 34

MOVING ON

R omeo sat on the couch, waiting. What was taking her so long to return from work? Images of Alessandra flashed before him. The way she tilted her head when processing ideas, the way her eyes steered to the side as she was thinking, the way her head remained high even during times of sadness. She was in his mind, morning and night, and he had to figure out how to shake her out of his life.

Once this villa was complete, he could move on. He could travel to Germany in the next couple of months and be done with Alessandra. She was still fresh in his mind because they worked together, but after that, she'd become a distant memory and would no longer linger in his brain. If only he could make her understand that he hadn't been using her physically. He respected her.

His phone rang out with a video call. Adriana appeared on the screen. "Hey, Romeo."

One elbow rested on the edge of the couch. "This is a surprise. What's new?"

Adriana tilted her head. "You don't look well. Have you been sleeping?"

He sighed, not needing to be mothered. "Not really. Too much to do with this villa."

"I am worried about you, bro. It's Alessandra, isn't it? You've fallen for her and are probably too stubborn to admit it." He remained silent. "Why don't you talk to her?"

He glared at the screen. "I talk to her every day." How could his sister be so astute about his current state? He believed it would be out of sight, out of mind.

She shook her head. "You get what I mean, Romeo."

"And say what, exactly?"

She sighed. "You idiot. That you're in love with Alessandra."

He shook his head, not wanting to admit he had strong feelings for her, but love, no. It couldn't be, could it? She was exciting, beautiful, and smart, and he missed their banter and the sex, but he would forget about her soon enough. "Ridiculous, Adriana."

She crossed her arms. "Then why do you glance away every time I mention her name? Why do your eyes light up like a Christmas tree whenever you talk about her? Explain it to me like I'm a five-year-old, Romeo."

"I already explained it you, sis. I don't need to rehash this. In fact, I've accepted an offer to work in Germany after this project. It is another opportunity for my career."

She squinted. "Are you for real? Why are you running away? Don't you need to return to your life, your home? Come on, Romeo. You're thirty, not a twenty-year-old anymore. It is time to settle down." His shoulders deflated. "Why are you letting your past cloud your judgement? Not everyone is like Diana. Can't you distinguish the two? For one, Alessandra didn't cheat on you when you were together, and two, from what you told me, she is the exact opposite of your ex-fiancée. But because you're afraid to feel, you're giving up on her."

"I am not talking about this anymore. Tell me about you and the family. How is everyone? How's mum?"

"She is fine, but don't use that damn tactic on me. We need to finish this."

He listened to her drone on until she got tired of it, then ended the call. He was tired of his one-track mind.

Alessandra crept into the apartment and aimed for the kitchen after Giuseppe dropped her off. She opened the fridge and found a plate of left-over risotto for dinner. She'd had a relaxing coffee with Giuseppe in the local café, and they'd talked mainly about his family and his upcoming projects. He kindly steered clear of talking about Romeo.

Pulling out the plate of risotto from the microwave oven, she sat down and chewed on the cheesy, rich flavours—a meal that Romeo had made yesterday. The man could cook.

Footsteps drew her eyes up. Pale faced, Romeo had dark circles under his mirthless eyes. "You're late. Where were you?"

"I went out for coffee with Giuseppe. We had a nice time."

He sat across from her, clasping his hands in front of him. "What did you talk about?"

"Mainly about his family and his upcoming projects. He sure is proud of his children, in spite of them giving him grey hairs at times. He has a big heart and reminds me of my Dad. What were you up to?"

He shrugged. "I was finalising a few details with Mike on the phone. Taking part of the day off put me a little behind."

She forked a slice of mushroom. "Giuseppe mentioned you weren't feeling well. Are you okay?"

He sighed, the minutes of silence awkward between them. "Only tired. I haven't been sleeping and rested a little on the couch. I did manage a few hours of sleep, but napping during the day impacts my night."

"I am glad you got some much-needed rest." She chewed more vegetables then took a sip of water. "I'd like to apologise for what I said earlier to the reporter. I didn't mean anything by it."

He sighed. "It's fine."

She looked into her plate, blushing. She gulped her water. It was at the end of the road with this project and she needed closure before they parted ways. "I am sorry if I upset you."

He nodded. "We all have our demons. I might be controlling, but I would never hurt you, at least not intentionally." He feigned a smile and got up. "I have to organise a few things in my room. I will talk to you tomorrow."

When he left, she wondered if things would ever be right between them. Were they going to leave without being on good terms?

Chapter 35

THE VILLA OPENING

One evening, three weeks later, Flavio and Giuseppe cut the ribbon tied up from one post to another.

"Here is to the grand villa with its beauty, impeccable charm, rustic-yet trendy design, and my new, magnificent, temporary abode while I work on my next film here in Montepulciano," said Flavio. "I have to thank each and every one of you for your hard work and catering to my every need. Thank you so much from the absolute bottom of my heart."

Alessandra had a spring in her step as she viewed the completed villa. The outdoor lights gave the villa a cosy ambience in the middle of the mountains. A bushy tree stood in front of the small cottage in the grounds, a set of wooden chairs and tables sat out front, and potted plants lined the side of the villa. She had relished working on the cottage, which was similar to the main house, yet cosier.

Casting deep shadows, the glow from the house's lights cut the darkness of early night, forming a chiaroscuro effect on Romeo's features as he stood beside her. She drank in his profile, memorising each feature as it was likely the last time she would see him.

Marguerite held her notepad, and stood to the side of her cameraman. "Tell us about the villa. Entice us."

Giuseppe put his hands together. "I commend Alessandra, Romeo and all the contractors for the excellent work they have done. The villa has five bedrooms, with a grand rustic sitting room, a bar and billiards area, a gym, and a cosy library with a fireplace. We have a kitchen and an indoor games room ready for entertaining. The sliding door in the living area will eventually feature a landscaped garden and possibly a hammock, but the interior is all complete."

After Flavio's first official tour of the villa, Alessandra took a moment for herself to stroll the grounds, stopping to rest on a bench beneath a tree. She imagined what it would be like to not see Romeo every day. They'd been working together for the past six months, and she knew she would miss him. She would never admit it to him and never again make the mistake of involving herself with anyone on a casual basis. Her heart was big and as much as she hated to admit it, she was in love with Romeo, but it could never work between them. Not when he didn't love her in the same way. Sure, he might have cared about her, but it wasn't enough to sustain a long-term relationship. She deserved a man who could love her, and was determined to put him out of her mind forever.

Romeo approached and stood beside her. "The others would like you to come inside and say goodbye. Don't you have a flight at midnight?"

"I do, and I will come now." She got up, yearning to reach out to him for a final kiss or a final hug.

He reached for her and wrapped his arms around her. "I am going to miss you, Alessandra. Can I call you when I return from Germany?"

Had he changed his mind about them? "Why?"

"I'd like for us to be friends at least. Who knows about the future?"

"I want commitment, Romeo. Are you telling me you feel differently now? You won't be back to Melbourne for another six months after Germany. Am I meant to wait for you?"

"I would like to keep in touch, Alessandra. Why can't we meet up then and see where things lead? I can't promise you anything, but maybe..."

"Maybe what?"

He swallowed. "I don't know, Alessandra. But it hurts to say goodbye. I cannot imagine my life without you in it. We've been working together for the past six months, and I will miss that. Won't you?"

"Life goes on, Romeo. And I will adapt as you will. Enjoy your time in Germany."

She turned away from him, and he reached for her hand, but she moved it away. "Wait, Alessandra."

"What?"

"I am trying to give you an olive branch here, and you're not meeting me halfway. I am telling you I would like to see where things go. It's all I can offer you right now. Maybe not a commitment, but a possibility of one in six months."

She wanted to be sick. He expected her to put her life on hold. "If you don't know how you truly feel, then goodbye, Romeo."

"I do care about you, Alessandra. Please know that."

She pushed down her fury and stepped back. "It's not enough. Goodbye, Romeo." Scurrying away from him, she squared her shoulders and entered the kitchen.

Romeo sat on the bench, looking into his shaking hands. His heart broke in two at the thought of not seeing Alessandra again. The problem was he was totally in love with her, but he couldn't commit to her, knowing he was a person who liked control. She deserved better than that. In the end, he knew she would hurt him, so this way, he was protecting his heart. But why did he mention meeting up in six months? Did he expect her to wait for him, when no doubt, she'd have her pick of men who would be more worthy of her than he was? No, he couldn't offer her a commitment, and realised that it could never work between them.

He bowed his head and tried to ignore the deep pit inside his stomach.

Giuseppe joined him on the bench. "Hey, Romeo. What are you doing out here?"

He lifted a shoulder. "I needed alone time."

Giuseppe squeezed his shoulder. "I can tell you're in love with her. Let me tell you a story about Enza and I."

He turned to him. "I know your story about your deep, abiding love and meeting on the train. What's there to tell me?"

He waved him away. "I too loved Enza like no-one else, but I let my pride stop me. I was afraid she'd break my heart so I had to break hers first. I considered I wasn't good enough for her. She was an educated woman who went to college, and I was just a lowly builder who didn't have any academic knowledge whatsoever. I didn't believe I could stimulate her intellectually, even when we talked all the time about everything. I never saw myself as smart, but she reminded me that I have a different kind of smart and that we had a lot in common. I knew that love was a risk but there were no guarantees in anything."

"It's a nice story, but it hardly compares to ours."

He chuckled. "You're wrong. You love Alessandra, but because of what she's been through with her ex-boyfriends and mother, you believe you're going to hurt her like they did. You feel unworthy of her. In the beginning, you made an excuse about your ex-girlfriend hurting you, but later it stopped being about her. It became about you. Why deny a love that is so rare, especially with a woman who has a huge heart and would never intentionally hurt anyone, let alone you?" Giuseppe gave him a reassuring smile then walked back inside the villa.

Romeo knew that he was an idiot, but now it was too late.

Chapter 36

MELBOURNE ARRIVAL

Romeo's eyes darted around the congested Florence Airport later that night. Earlier, Mike and Giuseppe had encouraged him to catch up with her to tell her how he felt before she left. He had missed saying goodbye to her when Marguerite asked him more questions about the villa. If only the traffic hadn't made him so late. It was past midnight when he looked through the boarding window as the aeroplane slowly took off. *No! I just missed her.* Now he couldn't tell her how he truly felt. He had lost her.

Not long after she left, he had tried calling her twice. But she had ignored his calls, and he couldn't blame her. If only he could have spoken to her before she left.

He'd been a right bastard to her. Taking a seat, he unfolded an addressed note in his hand and bowed his head, resolved to call her once she arrived in Melbourne. Maybe they had a chance, but he would have to make it up to her first.

Alessandra wrapped her arms around Mimi as she reached the arrivals lounge of the Tullamarine Airport. "I have missed you these past couple of months, Mimi."

"And I have missed you too." She pulled away, scanning Alessandra from head to toe. "Girl, you have lost weight."

Alessandra pressed her lips together. "I haven't had much of an appetite."

Mimi nodded. "Hmm. You will be fine once you're back in a routine. I've got your back, girl."

They ambled to baggage claim and waited. Thankfully, Mimi hadn't brought up the subject of Romeo. He had called her twice, but she couldn't talk to him and hear his lame excuses anymore. They were done. The quicker she forgot all about him, the better.

Chapter 37

EPILOGUE (TWO WEEKS LATER)

Alessandra locked her front door, and with keys in hand, she took a moment, lifting her head to soak in the warm sunlight streaming over her. Her car was parked at the kerb but she stopped short when her phone buzzed. Checking the message, she cursed to herself. *Why is he ringing me again? What's the point?*

Over the past couple of weeks, she had taken leave from work and spent time visiting her family, socialising with Mimi and her other friends, and planning her future business. During that period, Romeo had called her several times but she had ignored his calls. It was over between them, so what more could he say to rub salt in her wounds? She still pined for him but would be just fine as soon as he stopped calling and faded into her memories.

Right now she needed to buy groceries at the store and was planning to return to work next week. For now, she was relishing her relaxation time after the gruelling six months in Italy.

She reached her car and pulled at the handle.

"Alessandra."

Turning, she saw Romeo with a grim expression on his face. His eyes looked bloodshot yet soft as he took a step forward from across the footpath.

"What are you doing here? Shouldn't you be in Germany?" Her heart burned inside her chest and she pressed a hand against it as if she could keep down the tumult of emotion.

"You are a hard woman to track down. I went to your work but your boss said that you're on leave. I forgot the number of your street, so I asked around and knocked on a lot of doors to find you until your neighbour mentioned you living here."

Alessandra's throat constricted. "Why would you go to so much trouble?"

Romeo put up his hand. "I love you, Alessandra. I was too stubborn and scared to say it before, but I know now that I loved you from the first moment I saw you. It took me many months to realise that what we have is special, and I'd like us to be together, committed. I want to cherish you, love you, and be with you for as long as you'll allow." Alessandra's spine chilled, her mind clouded with so many questions. Did he think he could just show up here and have her bow down to him after all this time? She got up and returned to the front door, unlocking it. She faced him. "I will give you five minutes inside and then you need to leave."

He nodded sullenly. "Okay. Five minutes."

As they made their way to her living room, she noticed his eyes darting around her home, surveying the modern mahogany décor, ottoman, and L-shaped white leather sofa. "Take a seat."

"You have a beautiful home, Alessandra."

After waiting for him to sit at the end, she took her place at the other end. "You have four minutes." He scratched his palm. "Why, after all this time, should I believe what you say? You expect me to forgive you after the way you treated me back in Italy? You hurt me, Romeo, so much. And now you expect me to forget all that and act as if time hasn't passed? It has taken you almost seven months to commit to me. How do I know it is real this time? How do I know you won't just want a casual relationship again or nothing if things get too hard?"

He clenched his hands. "Because I have had time to gain a different perspective. I spoke to Giuseppe, who told me his love story. He made me realise I was scared. I thought I would hurt you, and I was scared you would hurt me because I can tend to be controlling and thought you might resent me later. Giuseppe gave me a new perspective on that last day, but I was too late to stop you. Your plane was gone. It might have taken me longer to be ready, but Alessandra. I always loved you. I never knew consciously at the time but it was there from the start. I love you so much it hurts."

His words drew her like a magnet. "What about Germany?"

"I turned down their offer and have been working in Melbourne. I started on the mental health centre, and Flavio is still on board."

"I don't know if I can trust you, Romeo. You had chances and you blew them."

His lips parted. "Do you love me, Alessandra?"

Her heart burned and ached inside, her breath catching on the lump in her throat. "Don't think that a few fancy words can fix this. If you loved me, you should have told me earlier. It's too late now." She rose and stomped to the door. Before opening it she hesitated. Was she doing the right thing sending him away? What if she lost him forever? But no, she was still fuming inside. He couldn't expect a few words to eradicate the last six months. "You should go now." Her legs threatened to betray her, but she was determined to get through this with her dignity intact.

Romeo's brows furrowed as he lowered his head. Colour drained from his face. "I am so sorry, Alessandra." He rummaged in his pocket and held out a piece of folded paper. "I was holding on to this a few weeks before you left Italy. I couldn't find the right time to give it you. This is your mother's address and phone number. An Italian friend of mine found it for me. She's still in Pisa. No pressure. Do with it what you will, but life is too short. I met with her in Pisa before I left and she wants to speak to you."

Her hands clasped over her mouth and her lip quivered. Whispering to hide the emotion, she said, "Thank you." He met with her? What was she like? What had he said? This was all too much. She felt at the edge of her control. Shaking, she grabbed the door handle and opened the door, standing aside to send a clear message and focusing on the tile beneath her feet.

He inched near her and lovingly touched her shoulder. "Tell me how you feel, then I will go."

Not trusting her voice, she slowly shook her head. Removing his hand, her shoulders deflated.

"Do you love me as much as I love you? I won't leave until you tell me." He exhaled. "If you love me, I will keep trying until you're ready. Even if it takes a lifetime."

A barely stifled cry cracked her voice, and she said, "Yes, dammit. I have always loved you and wanted you. The casual relationship was good for a while, but I wanted and needed more. Every night I think about you, but I knew I'd eventually get over you."

His heart lifted at this symbol of hope. "Will you give me a chance? Give us a chance?"

A sob caught in her throat and the tears streamed down her cheeks. As he gently smoothed them away, Romeo's eyes became glassy. He ran his hand through her hair.

Alessandra could no longer resist the painful yearning inside of her. She leaned in and closed the gap between them, embracing him. "I'm scared, Romeo."

Arms encircling her, he whispered, "Me too." She moved to put distance between them, but he wouldn't let her out of his arms and confessed, "I have craved you these past weeks without you around me. My chest burned. I couldn't sleep and eat. I am committing to you and to this new relationship we can build. I love you so much, Alessandra, it hurts."

She nodded. "I love you too, Romeo."

He cupped her neck and crashed his lips into hers, kissing her until the room spun away from her and the sobs of pain turned into a desperate desire within her. Breaking their kiss, he whispered, "Today will be the beginning of the rest of our lives." And he was right.

Reviews are GOLD to authors. If you enjoyed this book, please consider leaving Lucy a review.

Check out my other stand-alone romance novel, *Second Chances* here: http://mybook.to/Secondchances

ABOUT THE AUTHOR

Lucy Appadoo is a prolific reader and author of the Friends In Crisis Series. After a childhood spent reading and imagining escapist worlds, Lucy has put her imagination into stories. Her work as a rehabilitation counsellor, and former work as a counsellor in private practice, have led to an interest in writing inspirational stories about authentic, driven women who manage adversity with strength and heart. She writes in the genres of romantic suspense/thrillers with significant life themes and contemporary romance.

Lucy's interests include researching crime stories and news to inspire her work, watching crime thrillers and suspenseful movies, travel, exercising, reading for entertainment or knowledge, meditation, and spending time with friends and family. She also appreciates her Italian background and culture, which has inspired her to write imaginative stories about her parents' childhoods, leading to The Italian Family Series novels.

Check out Lucy's website and sign up for a FREE book here: https://www.lucyappadooauthor.com.au

ALSO BY LUCY APPADOO

Contemporary Romance – Stand-alone

Second Chances: http://mybook.to/Secondchances

Women Of Strength Series – Romantic Suspense

In Rio's Shadows (Book 1): https://books2read.com/u/mq1qP8

Shadows Of The Past (Book 2): https://books2read.com/u/3y1yAl

The Friends In Crisis Series – Romantic Suspense

Haunted By The Past (Book 1): https://books2read.com/u/bw2ZeY

Twisted Obsession (Book 2): https://books2read.com/u/4DW8pk

Web Of Lies (Book 3): https://books2read.com/u/3JXazE

Love-Obsessed (Book 4): https://books2read.com/u/4jPKGX

The Hearts Series - Romantic Suspense

Rising Hearts (Book 1): https://books2read.com/u/mZwpoE

Forbidden Hearts (Book 2): https://books2read.com/u/bQBKr7

Kindred Hearts - (Book 3): https://books2read.com/u/4AJKQK

Broken Hearts (prequel to Forbidden Hearts):

https://books2read.com/u/mgrnOD

Short Story Thrillers
Evening Interrupted: https://books2read.com/u/3yZDjZ
The Dreamcatcher: https://books2read.com/u/bzaLxn
Red Flags: https://books2read.com/u/bWZ9W1
Collection of Short Story Thrillers:
https://books2read.com/u/bP5vwj

The Italian Family Series - Coming of Age Family Drama/Romance
A New Life: https://books2read.com/u/mqqwZm
The Beauty of Tears: https://books2read.com/u/bpqwk3
Dancing in the Rain: https://books2read.com/u/bOr7LA
A Life By Design: https://books2read.com/u/3J8ene

NON-FICTION
Grief & Loss
Moving Beyond Grief - How To Shift From Grief & Loss to Joy & Peace: https://books2read.com/u/mVNzDA

Stress Management & Anxiety
Holistic Spiritual and Mental Health - Building Resilience and Creativity by Conquering Anxiety and Managing Stress: https://books2read.com/u/47kG8A

Career Guidance
Your Holistic Career Path - Create Career Change, Satisfaction, and Work/Life Balance: https://books2read.com/u/bzYDz4